Another Hood Love 3

by

Jontu

Text **LEOSULLIVAN** to 22828 to join our mailing list!

To submit a manuscript for our review, email us at leosullivanpresents@gmail.com

Chapter 1: Big Money Q

Dolo: *Ya girl out here wildin' man we was having fun for a minute but she just got into a fight with Lo, now we're sitting at the Marina getting high.*

Me: *Aight man. Tell her crazy ass to hit me up later on. I'll be out there in a few days.*

I shook my head as I placed my phone on my desk and logged into my email account. I checked over a few documents but I couldn't really get focused. Jaeda was clouding my brain and it was hard to shake her ass. It had been almost two years since I had met her and since the first time that I was in her presence, I had been on her line. She had been on the wild side since the death of her son and I wanted her to calm down and stay focused but as long as she was fucking with that bitch Loren, she would stay acting out. I had tried talking to her all the time about calming down and getting her life together but Jae was stubborn as hell, she did what she wanted when she wanted. Jaeda had her own money, her own home and plenty of cars but I wanted more for her. All that stuff was good but at the end of the day in the world we lived in, she would be just another uneducated black woman with expensive shit but nothing accomplished.

Jae was smart as hell, she was a whiz with numbers and money and she could talk herself out of anything. She just needed to get her head right because she could really be great at whatever she put her mind to.

I gathered all my things and placed what I needed inside my MCM bag. I was done for the day but I still needed to make sure that the shop was stocked with ink, needles and everything else it needed. I had already checked in with my other two shops and the café and they were straight with their supplies. This shop was my biggest headache. Out of all my shops, it seemed as though my employees at this shop were lazy and incompetent. I didn't mind them having fun every once in a while but I was going to clean house as soon as I got back because I couldn't be losing money trying to keep the niggas that I fucked with employed. Friends or not, this was a business and not a playground.

I owned three tattoo shops, two in Las Vegas and one in the Bay Area along with a café off of the Las Vegas strip. Big Ink was my biggest accomplishment. I was a street nigga that had come from a rough city and I had turned my life around and made something of myself. Before I had opened my first shop, my cousin Dolo and I used to run up in houses, stores, trap spots and whatever else in order to get that paper. We weren't getting small paper either. We would get the drop on the niggas with the big money or product and hit their ass. We had a good run for a cool five or so years, until one night shit just went all the way bad and that was the turning point for me. I'd almost lost my life and could have done some serious time in jail and that was the moment that I realized that God didn't give too many chances, so I counted my blessings and turned that money into something that would bring me longevity and not death.

I walked into the front waiting area of my shop and looked around. I shook my head as my assistant Grace sat on the phone bumping her gums while my shop was looking a mess and unorganized. It was the end of the day and we had the bulk of our customers early in the day but tomorrow was Friday and the weekends were chaotic.

I walked up to her and snatched the phone out of her hand. "You want to make money or collect unemployment? I'm sure them Instagram likes won't get you too far," I said as she looked up at me like a deer in headlights.

"My, my bad, boss man," she stuttered as she got up and grabbed the broom and started sweeping up.

"Just get your work done before you feel like you can cat off on my dime. There's a fresh shipment in the back and I need all the rooms stocked with fresh materials, bathrooms cleaned and stocked and make sure the windows, *all* the windows, and mirrors get wiped down," I said as I walked off. I didn't much like being in her face for long.

Grace was a high maintenance, overconfident bitch with a big booty, mediocre titties and a cute face but let her tell it, she was the baddest thing walking. She had three kids by three different niggas that didn't even stay around long enough to let the ink dry on the birth certificates and she lived with her brother and his baby mama but collected welfare and child support for only one child. Every time I was in her presence for too long, she got a little too comfortable by flirting and getting a little too touchy feely. I was doing my nigga Ace a solid by letting her work in my shop. She was his younger sister and at 22, the bitch was lazy and nothing but trouble and I wasn't trying to fall into that trap at all.

I fucked a few thots and shit but I would pass on that one. I didn't need the trouble that would come creeping around on my broad with her. My girl was crazy and I let bitches know off top because I ain't want to be the reason nobody got caught off guard. It was easier to not even fuck around sometimes; these bitches were hardly worth the trouble.

I counted out $500 and sat it on the counter for Grace and walked out of the building. I still needed to run to the cleaners to pick up my clothes and stop by the bank before I went home to pack for my flight. I hopped in my blacked out F-150 and pulled my phone out before I pulled off. I shot Jaeda a text and then threw my phone on the passenger seat. I couldn't wait to get back to the Bay. It had actually been almost two months since I had been and I was due for a break. I was trying to convince Gio to go on a trip but they had just given birth to their second child not too long ago and he wasn't trying to budge. That nigga needed to strap up because his ass was never ready to go on a vacation when it was time to. I drove towards the bank first as I nodded my head to Migos. I actually liked them little niggas. At first I couldn't stand listening to their music but they got some hits.

I looked over and noticed that my phone was ringing so I cut down my music and answered it. "Ric Gotti! What's good, baby?" I asked Rico. My nigga had only been home for about two months and I was glad that he was back. He had sat down for three and came back like he had never left. Jaeda and the rest of the Gas Squad, along with Dolo and I, had made sure that he didn't want for a thing while he was behind the wall. So when he came home, he took his money and flipped it and was now the owner of two hookah lounges. They weren't fully up and running yet but he had signed all the paperwork and the construction was now underway.

"Shit, what's good with my brother, though? When you touching the Bay?"

I chuckled as he said that because I hadn't seen my bruh since he got out and we were overdue for a turn up. "I will be there first thing in the a.m., my nigga. My flight lands at 11 and Dolo supposed to come swoop me so holla at that nigga so you can ride with him," I said as I pulled into the bank parking lot.

"Aight. Bet, I'll see you tomorrow, nigga." We hung up and I got out and headed inside the bank to make these deposits.

Chapter 2: Dolo

I looked over at Jae's face as we sat at the Marina on the hood of my old school, passing a blunt back and forth. I was really concerned about my little sis. Over the last two years, we had gotten so close and I really wanted only what was best for her but I knew that she would have to find her way on her own. Jaeda was only 20 years old and she was trying to find her path. She had been through a lot in her life and I knew that I would probably never understand how she felt or the pain that she endured every night when she went to sleep but I just wanted her to get it together.

Right now she was at the point where she was partying all the time, traveling and doing who knows what when she went away. I thought that Rico would be able to get through to her once he came home but even he was having a hard time doing so. I just stuck close to her when I was in town and kept my eye on her because Jae was really a handful. I couldn't wait for Q to get out here tomorrow because she always came out of her dark place when he was around.

I really couldn't stand that bitch Lo, she was a bad influence and I had heard some hoe stories about her ass. Not even from when she used to be a stripper but now. The bitch was grimy and a bona fide slut. I didn't know what Jae saw in the bitch but as long as she was around, I wouldn't disrespect her but I for sure had my eye on her ass.

"I know you not ready to talk, sis, but you have to make some changes. You can't be out here getting your face fucked up fighting bitches and shit. That shit ain't worth it if you ask me. Anything that hurts you more than it helps you should be let go, feel me?"

I passed Jae the blunt and just watched her. She was quiet and hadn't said a word since we had pulled up. I could tell she was pissed off and I just couldn't understand why she would let certain shit get to her, especially when she didn't have to. Jae was paid out the ass but you would never know it. I mean, she kept herself dressed in some fly shit and she always had the flyest whips but she didn't floss hella hard like most youngsters with money. She was real subtle with how she did shit and she was always taking care of somebody else. I wished she would put some of that money to good use and open a business or two.

I looked at my phone as I texted Q. He would be out here tomorrow and we were all getting together to celebrate Rico's coming home and his new businesses. Gio and China had just given birth to their new baby not too long ago so we were all going to get together and have some fun. I just needed Jaeda to shake whatever it was that she was going through. I didn't need her drama spilling over into this weekend.

"You ready to bounce, Jae Money?" I asked. She didn't answer me, she just jumped off the car and walked over to the passenger's side and got in. I followed her lead and got in the car as well and pulled off. I had some moves that I needed to make because I wasn't going to be on no type of work shit for the next three days.

"Can you just drop me off at home? I rode with Lo today," Jaeda said as she leaned her seat back and dropped her shades over her eyes.

Soon as I dropped Jaeda off, I stopped by the tattoo shop to collect the cash deposits so that could go drop them at the bank and just to make sure everything was good. It wouldn't take long to do that stuff and it was good because I still needed to stop at the spot so that I could shower and change. I had a date with this little bitch that I had met a couple of weeks ago. She wasn't hella bad but she had a fat ass and she was kind of cute, no kids and she worked as a teller at Bank of America. It was whatever, though. I wasn't trying to wife the bitch. I would most likely take her to get some food, grab a bottle and go get a room. My only intentions were to dig up in her guts and show her what this dope do.

I wasn't fond of relationships. I wasn't really built for all that. It was all good for others and seeing my niggas with their broads and shit, but at the end of the day, I just like to come and go as I please and fuck whoever I feel. I didn't want to have to consider a bitch's feelings before I did shit or think about a bitch's stomach when I was ready to grab some food. Nah, I left that shit for the niggas who liked to court these bitches. I wasn't a gentleman, I was a real life hood nigga and I wasn't for these bitches. Money was my first objective and also my last but if a bitch came along and she caught my attention, I would squeeze her in when I felt the need. Bitches always said I was stuck up and shit but at the end of the day, the only thing a female could provide that I couldn't give myself was a deep throat and hot pocket to shove these ten inches of dope in. I couldn't care less what they thought of me. Shit, I was young, handsome and wealthy.

I pulled up to the shop and hopped out my whip. I looked over at the old white lady giving me the screw face I laughed as she hurried up and locked her doors when I walked past. I had pulled up blasting my music and I was playing Webbie "Keep Ya Head Up." I didn't give a fuck though. White people always felt like that about a nigga. I ain't hate them, though. Shit, it was just life.

I walked into the shop and went straight to the back. I bumped into Ashley soon as I hit the back room. "Damn, boo, you scared me," she said as I gripped her ass in her low cut jeans and bit her neck. "Ouch! Dolo, that shit hurt," she said as she pulled away from me and handed me the deposit bags.

"Shut yo crybaby ass up and make sure all the booths are stocked and clean before you lock up," I said as I walked back towards the front.

"Damn, Dolo. I can't get no dick tonight?" she asked.

I turned back around towards her and smirked. "Yea, make sure you have something hot to eat for me when I come through later on," I said and walked out of the shop. I had no intentions on going through that bitch's house tonight. I just didn't feel like hearing her thirsty ass keep begging me to slide through because had I said no, that's what her ass would have been doing.

Q would have hella shit to say if he knew that I had been fucking one of the shop employees but shit, every nigga couldn't be like him and just pass up pussy left and right. Niggas like him were built for relationships and I was built to fuck these hoes and leave them. I hopped back in my whip and peeled off headed to the bank. I looked at my watch and saw that it was a quarter to six. I hit the gas and slid into the bank's parking lot. I grabbed the deposit bags and hopped out to go take care of my business.

***

I pulled up in front of Johnna's spot and pulled out my phone. I had damn near forgot the bitch's name. It was a good thing she had saved her name in my phone and not me because I would have saved her under Phatty and been calling her something dumb like boo, bae or ma all damn night. Shit, I probably still would but at the end of the day, I didn't plan on keeping her ass anyway. I shot her a text and let her know I was outside.

I pulled a blunt from my ashtray and lit it as I took a pull and nodded my head to the music. I had been off Webbie for the past couple of days. On the real, I fucked with real nigga shit. Fuck all that trying to be a real man. I was a real nigga and I could give a damn about who had something to say about it. I had love for my people but if you weren't in my circle then you wouldn't get anywhere near my soft side.

After a few minutes, Johnna walked outside and hopped in my car. "Damn, you know a gentleman is supposed to come up and ring the bell?" she said and I exhaled the smoke that I was holding in my lungs. Damn, this bitch was already starting in and we hadn't even pulled away from the curb.

"Well, good thing I never claimed to be a gentleman. What's up, ma? You up for some Benni's?" I asked as I passed her the blunt.

"I don't smoke and yeah, I could go for some Benihana's," she said.

I turned the radio up and hit my blunt. I was thinking about this move that I needed to make before I went back to Vegas. Johnna reached over and turned the radio down and I looked at her like she was crazy. See, this is why I didn't do shit like this because bitches didn't know how to let a nigga just have their moment. I already knew she was going to do the shit that all girls do, ask twenty-one questions. I would feed her bullshit ass answers like I did all the rest of the hoes. At the end of the day, I couldn't be a complete asshole or I wouldn't get anywhere near the panties.

"So what do you do? You have kids?" she asked.

"I own a couple of tattoo shops and nah, I don't have any youngins."

She looked at me and had a small sparkle in her eyes. Bitches always thought that they had hit the jackpot when they ran across a nigga who didn't have any kids but shit, they were the biggest dogs out of all niggas because we ain't have no daughters to think about when it came to thinking about respecting these bitches and we didn't too much give a damn about your kids or babysitting issues. If you couldn't find a sitter, I was on to the next, plain and simple. We made small talk until we got to the restaurant. Once we pulled up, we hopped out and went inside. I knew she was expecting me to pull out chairs and hold doors open and shit but man, ain't nobody had time to try and do all that extra shit for some pussy I ain't even got yet. I was liable to do all this extra shit and then the pussy be trash. Fuck all that.

Chapter 3-Jaeda

I walked in the house and went straight in to my room. Soon as I got in my room, I stripped down to my birthday suit and walked into the bathroom and turned the shower on. I wrapped my hair up and stepped inside. I knew that my body would be sore as hell tomorrow. I needed to get my rest tonight because I knew come tomorrow morning that I wouldn't be seeing my bed for a few days. Q had texted me earlier and told me that his flight would be in before noon so I needed to get my ass up first thing in the morning and hit the nail shop because once everybody got together, it was about to be on. Rico had just come home and it was going to be good being around everybody. I couldn't wait until my bitch Lex finally touched down. She was on her last stretch and had less than a year before she would finally be home.

I let the water run over my body. I had scratches and a couple of bruises and I shook my head. I swear my life was a movie and I honestly didn't even know how I would fix it. I made the stupidest decisions sometimes and I knew that I needed to get it together but shit, I was living life right now. Chasing a dream I guess, because sex, drugs and violence had become life since my son had died, and that's really all I had going. I was tired of hearing motherfuckers lecture me about what I should and should not be doing. I mean shit, it was my life and until I was ready to change, I was going to do me. Q loved to tell me what I needed to do and how I was out here living reckless but he would never understand the demons I dealt with in my dreams. I loved and respected the man that Q was but shit, right now I couldn't be what he wanted me to be.

I jumped as I felt a cool breeze hit my back. I turned around as Lo was stepping into the shower with me. I rolled my eyes and turned back towards the water. I grabbed my loofah and shower gel and finished washing my body.

"So you just going to ignore me, Jae?" Lo said as she reached around me and grabbed my nipple. She rolled it between her fingers and I threw my head back as I felt her lips on my neck. It was hard being mad at this bitch. Her ass was hella insecure and was always trying to flex on me to where we ended up fighting and then she came and used sex to try to make me forget about why I was mad.

"You just be trippin', my nigga, and I don't have time to always try and validate your insecurities. Who wants to be with somebody that they always fighting with, Lo? You of all people know that I don't want to be dealing with nobody like that. I went through enough with Chris' ass to last me two lifetimes. I don't need that shit, bitch," I said as I pushed her hand away and stepped out of the shower. I walked into the room and sat down on the bed.

I grabbed my vanilla body oil out of my drawer and started rubbing it on my legs, I could hear Lo in the shower crying. I rolled my eyes because her ass was hella extra and always crying about some shit. She would get mad, scream and curse and act all tough and then I would have to beat her ass. Next thing I know, she was crying like I had been dogging her ass out. I wasn't falling for the shit tonight. Her ass was about to just be crying because I didn't have the patience to pacify her damn feelings tonight.

I slipped on an orange panty and bra set with some matching knee high socks and walked out of my room and into the kitchen. I grabbed a spoon and a tub of ice cream and settled on my couch as I turned on the television and turned it to *Ridiculousness*. About a half an hour later, Lo finally had brought her crybaby ass out of the room and came to sit down next to me. She threw her legs over me and fired up a blunt.

I looked at her for a minute and tried to think how I really felt about her. Lo told me all of the time that she loved me but I couldn't bring myself to feel that way about her. I mean, my love for her was as a friendship kind of love. Yes, we were in a relationship and she damn near lived with me but she was sort of just something to do at the moment. The sex was crazy and she was fun to party with but I wasn't trying to be on no love shit with her or anybody, for that matter. On some real shit, I wasn't into females but some of the things that Lo did to me in the bedroom or shit, even in public on impulse could make my eyes roll back and toes curl for days.

That last night in Miami, I had fallen asleep talking to Q and when I woke up, my panties were around my ankles and my pussy was wetter than a faucet. My initial thought was that Q was in between my legs, but when I opened my eyes and saw Lo down there, I was stuck. I didn't know what to do. I guess I sort of was blinded to all of the little advances she had made before and I just played it to the left thinking I was tripping. I wanted so bad to stop her that night because I knew that crossing that line was going to change everything but I was so high and her tongue felt like silk on my pussy so I couldn't stop that shit for nothing. I was determined to feel what the ending was going to be like. She had licked me from my ass to my belly button and the shit was amazing. After we got back from Miami, I had avoided her ass for a whole week. She called and texted all day, every day and then one night, she just showed up and once I let her in, she was on me like white on rice. I didn't really know what to do but one thing led to another and here we were. Lo had turned the fun and sex into something more than it was. I didn't know where this shit was going but I couldn't continue to fight with her because she was insecure.

She took a hit from the blunt and then leaned in and pressed her lips to mine, giving me a charge. I accepted it and inhaled the smoke into my lungs. I sat back and grabbed the blunt from her and hit it twice before laying my head back on the back of the couch. Lo stood up and dropped to her knees as she grabbed my panties and pulled them off my legs. I pulled my knees up and opened them wide. This was nothing new, we argued and fought and then she tried to make it up by giving some fire head. I wasn't turning down no head but I wasn't fucking with her, either. I told her time and time again that I wasn't dealing with that crazy ass, insecure bullshit and I could show her ass better than I could tell her.

I watched Lo as she plunged her thick, warm tongue inside me as far as it would go. She wrapped her lips around her tongue and I could feel them on my flesh as she swirled her tongue around inside of me. Every time she plunged back in, it was like soft kisses on my lips. "Shit!" I moaned as she pulled her tongue out and began to suck on my clitoris roughly as she stuck two manicured fingers inside of me and began stirring my honey pot. I began to grind into her face as she picked up the speed and began to lick her tongue around my outer lips. I grabbed her face and held it tight as I threw my legs over her shoulders and I thrust my pussy in her face.

Lo stared deeply in my eyes as she was being smothered in my sweet cream. She began to go hard and eat my shit like it was her last meal. I closed my eyes and let the powerful feeling take over as my pussy began to squirt. Lo didn't back down, though. She accepted every drop and then licked me clean. I dropped my legs and pushed her back as she tried to rub on my pussy some more. I know I was being rude but I wasn't feeling her ass right now.

"Damn, bae, you ain't going to let me finish?" she asked as she reached again to touch me.

I grabbed her hand and pushed it back. "Nah, I'm straight." I got up and headed for the kitchen to throw away the empty ice cream container and grab a bottle of water. I placed the spoon in the sink and turned around to find Lo standing behind me with my phone in her hand.

"See what I mean? Every time I turn around, this nigga or the next is hitting you up trying to chill or some shit!" Lo yelled at me. I just grabbed my phone and brushed past her ass. I didn't have time for this. "So you ain't got shit to say? Just fuck me, huh?"

I turned around and she already had tears streaming down her cheeks. I rolled my eyes and walked closer to her. "Look, Lo, I don't know what the fuck you

24

expect me to say to your insecure ass. I'm grown as fuck and I make my own money and pay my own bills and yours. I can do as I damn well please and I ain't got to answer to anybody. You the one that turned what we had into a relationship. I didn't want to commit to nobody but you're the one who makes yourself mad and cry when you should just be riding the wave and having a good time!" I yelled, frustrated with all the bullshit that came with this bitch.

"You said you didn't want a relationship with another nigga!"

I laughed and stared at her for a second to see if she was serious. "Bitch, what? I don't fuck with females so you just thought that was your invitation to come and turn me out, because I said I didn't want a nigga? What we got is fun and exciting for now but I can't build a life with you. I'm not set up like that. You may be in love but bitch, I ain't. So now you can get your mind right and be here when I get back or you can do you and cut!" I stood there staring at her for a moment as I watched her watch me.

"So you about to go chill with that nigga Sherrod?"

I just shook my head and walked away. I was praying that bitch cut because I was too close to beating her dumb ass for the second time today. I went upstairs and washed up in the bathroom and then threw on a pair of leggings with no panties and a hoodie with some all-white Dunks. I grabbed my phone and wallet and got up out of there.

I didn't even plan on kicking it tonight. I had just wanted to relax but Lo had pissed me off so bad that I just needed some air. I knew I had hurt her feelings but I really didn't even give a fuck. I was tired of tiptoeing around the truth and the only way to not get anything misconstrued any further than it already was to just be real. It had been almost two years but the last six months she had just clung to me. At first, it was all fun and free but I guess she caught feelings. Don't get me wrong. I fucked with Lo the long way but on some real shit, I wasn't even gaining anything by fucking with her. She wasn't putting in any work when I was out in the streets. I splurged on her and took her on trips, bought her cars and loaned her money that I never asked for back so if she wanted to cut, I wouldn't be mad. I would be losing a friend but also ending a headache.

I pulled up to Sherrod's apartment and honked my horn as I waited for him to come out. I had met Sherrod at school and after Baby Tone passed away, I was struggling in my classes and I would pay him for the answers to the tests. Outside of school, we had also gotten really cool, he was a major party animal and hella cool to hang with. Plus, his tongue was golden.

He and I had never actually had sex but he would occasionally ask to taste me and shit, I would let him. I wasn't returning the favor, though. Nor was I going to have sex with him. I hadn't had actual sex with a guy since Chris, but I had fooled around with a few niggas since then. I would usually just get some neck and cut. When I was high, I just really loved the way lips felt on me but it had been two years and I was in need of the real thing but I just wasn't trying to give it up to anybody. I wasn't just super innocent but I wasn't just doing hella shit either. Most times Lo was always around me and we ended up together anyway so I didn't creep off much.

I looked up as Sherrod climbed into my passenger seat. "What's up, Jaeda? Where's your warden at?" he asked as he chuckled.

"Hopefully packing her shit." I got out and went inside the trunk of my car and pulled out a bottle of Patron along with a baggy full of mollies that I had stashed. I climbed back into the car, opened the bottle, broke open four capsules and poured them into the bottle of Patron.

"Aight, party girl. I see you, nigga, but damn you and Lo fonkin' that hard for her to leave?"

I looked at him and shook my head. I wasn't going to go all into what it was because it wasn't his business. "Yeah, we're just not on the same page so if she's there when I come home, then whatever and if not, then that's cool too. But fuck all that. Where are we going? You know I grabbed my ID."

Sherrod turned on the navigation and I began to drive. I pulled up to a bar and looked down at my attire. "Bruh, please, it's a bar and it's only Thursday. You good," Sherrod said, seeing my hesitation.

I put my phone in my glove box and locked my car as we walked into the small bar. It was most definitely smacking inside. I saw a few people I knew from school and waved. I was high as shit from drinking that Patron and I was feeling myself already. Sherrod grabbed a handful of my ass and steered me towards the back of the bar as we walked to the back. I was too high to even care about his public display of affection. We took a seat on the couch and Sherrod grabbed a bottle of Don Julio off the table and began to line shots up. I grabbed my shot and we tapped our glasses together and downed them at the same time. I was so high I couldn't even taste the alcohol because my tongue was numb. I smiled as my pussy tingled and I leaned over and grabbed my second shot.

"You better slow yo' ass down because if I see something up in here, I'm leaving yo' ass," Sherrod said as he took his second shot.

"Damn, how are you going to just abandon me for the next bitch?" I asked.

"Do you plan on giving me some ass?" I shook my head. "Exactly!"

I mushed him in the face and stood up and started dancing to the throwback Plies song that had just come on.

I opened my eyes and rolled over. I jumped up and looked around and I was confused. I looked at my watch and it said 7:23 a.m. I looked down and I was butt ass naked. "What the fuck?" I said out loud. I saw a lump in the bed next to me and lifted the cover. I covered my mouth and hopped out of the bed.

The person in the bed sat up and smiled. "Hey, are you okay?" he said.

I just stood there staring at him. I tried my best to remember last night but I couldn't remember shit. I had just climbed out of the bed with a white guy and I was puzzled. "Umm, no. actually, I'm not. No offense, but who the hell are you and did we…" I covered my face with my hands as I waited for him to answer my question.

He chuckled before he responded, "No, beautiful, we didn't have sex but you did let me taste that sweet chocolate that you have. But you passed out and I didn't think either of us were in any condition to drive home even though you drove here pretty well."

I let my hands drop from my face and I stared at him for a second. He was a tall white guy with dark brown hair and deep blue eyes. He had a nice athletic build and a small goatee. He was cute as hell for a white guy but I had never even thought about stepping outside of my race. I reached down and gathered my clothes and rushed into the bathroom. I couldn't believe the shit I had done. I didn't remember shit and I needed to get the hell up out of here. I hopped in the shower and washed up with the quickness. I threw my clothes back on and brushed my hair into a ponytail. I walked out of the bathroom, grabbed my things and walked smooth out of the hotel room. What the fuck was wrong with me? A damn white boy.

Chapter 4- Loren

I was livid as I packed up my stuff. It was after five in the morning and Jaeda had not come back home. She had left hours ago to go kick it with that pretty boy Sherrod. I knew they were fooling around no matter how much she wanted to deny it but they were way too comfortable around each other. I saw how he would be looking at her when he thought nobody was paying attention. He was a straight man and very good looking and they spent way too much time together for me to believe that they hadn't explored something before. I was always dealing with her being up under one nigga or the next, especially that nigga Q. The nigga had a whole ass bitch but every time I turned around, he was always sniffing up under mine. I was cool on all that disrespectful shit and I hoped these niggas played her ass like she had played me.

I was throwing everything in my bags. I knew it was wrong but I was even grabbing some of Jaeda's shit. She wouldn't even miss the shit because whatever was missing she would buy another one or not even notice it was gone. Shit, she had stacks on top of stacks in the bank and in her safe. I was throwing clothes and shoes, perfume, makeup and electronics in my bag. I couldn't believe the shit she had said. I had been here for her ass day in and day out and she basically told me that I didn't mean shit to her ass. I was done. I couldn't keep being here and letting her just stomp all over my heart because she felt like she could. Jaeda acted like she just didn't have any feelings. I knew she had been through a lot but you would think that after two years and being around somebody every day that she would have learned to love me like I needed her to.

She didn't have to trip, though. I still had my own spot and I would leave since it was clear that was what she wanted. I bet she would regret it once she realized what she had lost, but I was going to give her space and go do me. I was tired of not being loved like I needed. My mom never felt like I was good enough, my first love didn't and now Jaeda just felt like I was nobody. Fuck them all.

I walked into the bathroom and plugged up the tub. I turned on the hot water and let it run. I zipped up both of my bags and dragged them into the living room. I walked into the kitchen and reached behind the refrigerator and unplugged it. Jaeda had just gone grocery shopping and I was sure it would be a day or two before she even realized that her food had gone bad. I reached into the cabinet under the sink and grabbed the bottle of bleach and went back into her bedroom. I took a shirt and covered my mouth and nose and poured the bottle of bleach all over her bed. I was so mad that I was just doing anything that I could think of. So what I was being petty as hell. I opened the front door and dragged my bags out to my car. I looked down and grabbed one of the bricks in the walkway and walked over to the garage. I hit the clicker on my key ring and waited for the door to rise.

I stood there looking at all of Jaeda's precious whips and threw the brick at the front windshield of Jae's Maserati. I pulled my keys out and keyed the Masi as well as her truck. I ran back in the house and I was out of breath. That was how pissed I was. I stood in the middle of the living room and looked around. I looked up at the 70" TV that sat on the wall and threw the glass ashtray at it as hard as I could a huge crack spread through the screen and I smiled. I felt a little better but it would take me a few days before I wasn't mad anymore. I pulled Jaeda's house keys off my key ring and dropped them on the kitchen floor as I walked through it and grabbed a knife out of the utensil drawer. I turned on the water at the kitchen sink and plugged up the drain. I walked back out to the garage and flattened the tires on both of Jae's cars and walked to my car. Tears streamed down my face as I pulled out of the driveway. I called AT&T and had them change my phone number as I drove home.

Chapter 5- Dolo

I sat up in the bed and looked over at Johnna. Her drunk ass was knocked out and it was a little after 7 a.m. I leaned down and picked up my clothes as I walked to the bathroom in the hallway. I grabbed a washcloth from the shelf and washed up with the Dove soap in the shower. I had stayed longer than I had wanted but her uppity ass was a freak. She was doing all kinds of tricks and I ended up passing out. After I washed up, I threw on my clothes and grabbed my keys and phone off of her dining room table. I walked into the kitchen and opened the refrigerator. She had a jug of Simply Blueberry Lemonade so I grabbed it and walked out the front door. I was thirsty as shit. She would be alright and if she was tripping off that damn jug of juice then I would buy her another one and then leave her petty ass alone.

I hopped in my whip and rolled a blunt before I pulled off. I knew I wasn't about to go back to sleep so I decided to hit up Jaeda and see if she wanted to get some breakfast. I shot her a text and she surprisingly texted right back. I just knew her partying ass wouldn't respond for another hour. I told her to meet me at Denny's in half an hour. If she was already up then I knew she had possibly never gone to bed. I had to go and scoop up Rico before Q's flight landed so I had a little time to chop it up with sis. I pulled up to Denny's and hopped out. I walked in and waited for the waitress to acknowledge me.

"Eating alone?" she asked.

I frowned at her ass. "Nah, I'm waiting for somebody. Let me get that booth in the back by the window." This bitch was ugly as shit and she was trying to give me her best sexy face. She was squinting and smiling and the bitch was looking like a blind anteater. I wanted to laugh at her ugly ass but I was sure life was hard enough for her ass.

I ordered two orange juices then sat and watched the news as I waited on Jae to arrive. I shot Rico a text and let him know that I would be there around 10 to grab him so that we could make it to the airport. A couple of minutes later, I watched Jae walk towards me. Her eyes were bloodshot red and she was looking like she needed a nap.

"Damn, sis, you sure you ready for breakfast?" I asked. I reached in my pocket and handed her my Visine, she put two drops in each eye and passed it back.

Jae pulled Tylenol from her wallet and popped them in her mouth as she sipped her orange juice. I chuckled because her ass really needed to slow down. "Man, bruh, I need a vacation."

I nodded my head, "Who you telling? Me and Q were talking about hitting up Mexico for a week real soon. You down?" The waitress walked up and we both placed our orders, I wasn't even hella hungry but I knew I needed to coat my stomach before starting my day.

"Hell yeah, I'm down. You already know I love to get the hell up out of here," Jae said as she began to perk up a little.

Jae told me about the shit that had transpired between her and Loren and I was happy as hell inside. I was so tired of that needy ass bitch being around and I hoped she stayed her ass away. I wouldn't show Jae how I really felt because she was my sis and I tried my best to just be supportive but I swear that hoe was bad news and I hoped that she had cut. We finished up our food and I paid the bill. I looked at the time and it was only a little after nine.

"Aye, let me come shower at yo' spot, sis," I asked as we walked out to the parking lot. We were closer to her place than mine and I had some clothes in my trunk that I could change into.

"It's good. I was going to ride with y'all to go pick up Big Money Q anyway," she said as she giggled. We hopped into our cars and headed towards her house.

I put my car in park and jumped out of my car at the same time as Jaeda. Her garage door was wide open and we both stopped and stared at the scene before us. The words "Bitch" and "I hate you" were scratched into the paint of her Maserati and her Audi, the tires were flat and the front windshield was busted out.

"Damn, Jae, you must have really pissed that bitch off," I said as she shook her head and we walked in the house. Soon as we stepped into the kitchen, we looked down as water splashed at our feet.

"Oh, hell fucking no!" Jaeda yelled as she walked to the sink and turned off the water that had overflowed all over the kitchen floor.

I listened closely as I heard something coming from the back of the house. "The bathroom water is running, too," I said as I made my way into the bathroom to turn off the water in the bathtub. I reached in and unplugged the tub. There was water everywhere and I could hear Jae yelling and cussing. I walked to where she was and saw that her TV was cracked as well. I shook my head as Jae pulled her phone out and attempted to call Lo.

"This bitch changed her number. On God, when I see that hoe, I'm beating her ass!"

Jaeda went and grabbed an overnight bag and I called my boy at the BMW dealership to come and pick up both of Jaeda's cars. I then hopped on Google so that I could find somebody to clean up the water damage. I found a company and they were on their way.

Jae came back into the living room and placed her bag on the couch. She looked pissed. "Do you know that dumb bitch stole all my perfume and hella makeup? I am so pissed off."

I nodded my head as I grabbed her bag and walked out to the car. Jaeda was behind me and she was inspecting her cars. "Where ya keys at? We need to pull both cars out because Marcio from the dealership is sending somebody over to come pick them up. He said give him a week and they will be good as new," I said as we pulled the cars out and into the driveway.

"I think I want custom paint, since they are going to go to the shop anyway I might as well come saucy on they ass."

I laughed because her ass was like a nigga when it came to her cars. "Aight, well, you can go down there later and choose your paint before he sends them to the paint shop and the cleaning company is coming for the water. They should be here in fifteen. You know you can't stay here for at least two weeks, right?" I asked her.

She shook her head and I knew she was frustrated. Now females see what niggas go through fucking with these crazy ass hoes. Females get real childish when they get mad.

Everything at the house had been taken care of and we were running a little late. Jae and I hopped into my truck and pulled off to go snatch up Rico and go get my big cousin from the airport. We rode in silence for a minute. I grabbed my weed jar from under my seat and tossed it to Jaeda along with some blunt wraps. She was looking in need of a good blunt. I pulled up to Rico's house and told him I was outside. A couple minutes later, he hopped in. "

Sup with y'all?" he asked as he sat back and put his seat belt on.

"Shit, man. Jae Money got girl problems. That crazy bitch tore up her house and cars," I said, filling him in on the latest drama.

"Damn, Jae, you like a real nigga. Why you do Lo like that?" Rico asked, laughing. Jae even cracked a smile. I was glad the weed was doing its job and loosening her up because I hated being around her ass when she was grouchy.

I pulled up to the Southwest terminal at the Oakland Airport and was looking for my nigga Q. I didn't see him and the whack ass sheriffs were harassing people so I pulled off and went around again while Jaeda called him to see where he was.

"Jae, you juiced to be seeing your boo? You a single lady now so you ready to bust it open for my cousin?" I asked as me and Rico burst out laughing.

She looked at me and gave me the finger. "I ain't fucking with Big Money. I don't want to have to put hands on his bitch," Jaeda said as she popped a mint in her mouth. Yeah, she was feeling my nigga.

I pulled back up to the curb and spotted Q. I honked the horn and watched Jaeda as she stared at Q as he approached the truck. "Damn, sis, take a pic. It lasts longer," I said as I tried to block her punch. She was aggressive today. I laughed and hit the locks.

"Damn, y'all smoked up all the dro?" Q asked as he hopped in. I turned around and dapped him up.

Jaeda turned around in her seat to look back at him. "Nigga, don't get in this motherfucka' complaining before you even speak. It's too early for your bullshit!" Jaeda yelled.

I laughed as Q looked at me. "Man, give her a pass. It's been a long morning," I said as I pulled away from the curb.

"Well hello to you, Oscar the Grouch."

I shook my head. Jae and Q were going to go at it all damn day and I wasn't going to say shit else. I swear those two just needed to fuck and get over it. They couldn't wait to get around each other but then talked shit to one another the whole time.

"Dolo, stop by the mall. I need to grab some shit," Jae said as my phone began to ring.

I looked at the screen and smirked. My phone was connected to the car so when I answered the phone, the call came over the speakers. "Hello," I said as I placed the phone in my lap.

"Did you really take my bottle of lemonade, though?" Johnna asked with an obvious attitude.

I chuckled. "My bad, ma. I was thirsty as shit and I didn't think you would be trippin'," I said as I grabbed the blunt that Jaeda was passing to me.

"Boy, of course I'm trippin because it's my juice and I woke up thinking I was about to drink it. You are a real asshole, you know that? I can't believe your rude ass has such good dick."

I laughed as she went off on me. I thought about how wet and tight her pussy was and I was ready to jump right back into that shit. "My nigga, if you that mad I will bring you another bottle. I knew I should have left you a five in the fridge but check it out, ma. I'm with my family so I will get with you later on," I said before hanging up. I pulled into the mall and we all hopped out of the truck. I threw my arm around Jaeda. She was quiet on the ride over and I wanted to make sure she was good. "You straight, sis?" I asked as we walked inside the Nordstrom's entrance.

"Yeah, I'm good, Dolo. I think since I can't go home for a couple of weeks that we should take that trip to Cabo. I could use the getaway. I know y'all can't stay the full two weeks but I need to cut before I kill somebody."

I laughed as Jae's nostrils flared and a small vein poked out of her forehead. "Well, let's see what everybody else is talking about and we can book our flights and rooms once we're all on the same page," I said.

Q walked up and pushed my arm from around Jaeda's shoulders. "You looking mighty comfortable, my nigga," he said as he took a fake jab at me.

"Shit, comfortable or not, you better be cool before Laniece come jumping out the bushes on you with her crazy ass." We all started laughing. Q's broad Laniece was crazy as hell. She was the type of broad that tapped your phone and called *Cheaters* on a nigga.

On plenty of occasions, Laniece had shown up somewhere when we were out chilling and it didn't matter what city or state we were in. She would be blowing him up every hour trying to see what he was doing. I didn't see how niggas liked to put up with shit like that. Q didn't even love that bitch. I think he was just keeping time with her ass because he couldn't have Jaeda. Laniece wasn't even his type. She was a couple of years older than him and she was boring. Q didn't like boring bitches. She was the type that liked to stay in the house and read or have dinners with her parents and siblings for fun. She didn't like to travel or party unless she thought that Jaeda or some other females were coming along, then she was ready to tag along. She didn't have any kids and she was a paralegal for a law firm in Vegas. The bitch was dry and let Q tell it, he wasn't even trying to build a family with her.

We walked around as Jaeda was grabbing a few bottles of perfume from the fragrance counter. I looked at a few bottles but I didn't see anything that I wanted. I watched as Jae and Q flirted and fake argued back and forth and shook my head. Q needed to drop his lame ass bitch and snatch up Jaeda before she ended up making a mistake and ending up with somebody else that she shouldn't be with. After about an hour of walking through the mall, we each had at least three bags and were all ready to go finally.

Gio had already called to see where we were. He and China were barbecuing and we were supposed to have been there at one but it was already ten after 2. I looked down at my phone and replied back to a text from Ashley. She was pissed that she had cooked and I had never came through. She sent me a picture of a plate with some crab, salad and a shrimp and broccoli topped baked potato. The next picture she sent was a picture of her pussy as she was rubbing a whipped cream covered strawberry over it. My dick jumped in my pants at the sight. I made a mental note to slide through there tonight.

I texted Ashley back and apologized, giving her a fake story about going home and falling asleep. Just as I was putting my phone back in my pocket, I received another text. I pulled my phone back out and looked at the picture that had just downloaded. These hoes were wildin' out today. I smiled as I looked at the picture that was on my screen. I was trying to figure out how in the hell Johnna took the picture she had just sent because it was a pussy shot from the back, she was bent over spread eagle and that shit was looking right. I text her back and told her to keep it warm for me and then put my phone up.

Jaeda walked up on me as we got to the car. "What you over here smiling for?" she asked as we all got into the car.

I shook my head and looked at Jaeda. "Sis, these bitches be crazy!" I said, laughing. She laughed with me.

44

Once everybody was in the car, I pulled off and headed to Gio's.

Chapter 6: Jaeda

Mentally, I was exhausted as hell. I had made two horrible choices back to back. Like damn, what the hell is wrong with me? I didn't even know what even possessed me to even deal with a female, let alone my own friend. I was standing in the shower at Gio's in one of the guest bathrooms and I was just thinking about my life. It was a disaster and something had to shake because I couldn't keep taking losses. I had lost everything that mattered to me. The material things were nothing because everything destroyed could be replaced, and all of the things that Lo had destroyed were being replaced. I had already gone online and ordered a brand new bedroom set as well as living room furniture. I was getting custom candy on both vehicles but that didn't really mean shit because I had lost far more over the last few years. No amount of money could bring back my son, my sister or the love of my life.

I turned the water off and stepped out of the shower and then I grabbed my towel off of the towel rack and wrapped it around my body. I just stood there staring at myself through the fogged up mirror. As I stared at my reflection, I realized that my life was just like this foggy mirror. I could see what was there but I would never see it clearly until I cleared away all of the bullshit. I couldn't wait for somebody else to clear it away, I had to do it myself. So at that moment, I made a vow to myself to get my life together. Too many people depended on me and I couldn't keep fucking around and having so much bullshit around me.

I dried off and threw on my clothes. I just wanted to be comfortable so I was dressed down in a pair of light blue skinny Levi's, a long red cardigan with a black spaghetti strap shirt and a pair of black leather knee high riding boots. I threw on a couple of pieces of jewelry and some lip-gloss and I was all set. I went downstairs to where everybody else was and I was ready to just chill and have a good time without dwelling on the negative things in my life.

I walked into the kitchen and grabbed Charlie up in my arms as she ran out of the kitchen headed towards the living room. "Hey, Char-Char! Where you going, girl?" I asked as I kissed her chunky cheeks. She giggled and kissed me back on my cheek. I missed this little girl and I wished my son was here to play with her. They would have been so cute. At three years old, she was the spitting image of her daddy and it was adorable. I put her down and headed into the kitchen where I walked over to China and kissed her on the cheek. "Hey, China doll, what you need me to do?" I asked as she stood at the counter mixing contents in a large pitcher.

"Uh uh, hoe. Y'all late as hell. I don't need you doing shit now. everything is finished, wit' yo' ugly ass," she said pointing at me with the large metal spoon.

I scrunched my face up at her, "Girl, bye. You ain't got to be rude, bitch," I said, being hella extra with her ass.

She looked at me and smiled. "And you ain't got to be late, but you are! I'm going to call Lo and tell her next time she want to hold you up, y'all gone have to pay me."

I laughed at her crazy ass, "Well, if you talk to Lo, then tell that bitch to duck when she see me because I'm going to knock her head off."

China turned quickly on her heels and stared at me with questioning eyes. "Ooh, bitch, what happened now?"

I shook my head and grabbed the bottle of Don Julio off the counter top then I opened the bottle and poured her and me a shot. I stood there and ran down the events of the last two days, starting from the fight that we had on the block yesterday. I even told China how I woke up next to that cute ass white boy. After telling China everything, we had taken four shots each and I was definitely starting to feel the effects in my eyes and the back of my neck. I thought about the mollies I had but I quickly shook the thought off. I was trying to turn over a new leaf so I needed to drop some habits in order to get back right.

"Girl, that's some shit right there. Well, I hope you really done with that hoe because she ain't cool at all and when you see her ass, you better slide that bitch." I laughed because China was usually the quiet calm one but she could get real hood at times. I loved her ass like a sister and I hated that I had stayed away so long.

"What bitch are we sliding?" I turned around and laughed as Jamiya and Tamia walked into the kitchen together. I laughed at Jamiya's hyphy ass. She was always ready to get in to some trouble. If I ever needed somebody to handle something, she was always down.

"What's up with the hoes?" I asked as I poured the both of them a shot of tequila.

"Not shit, but what hoe do we have to drag?" Tamia responded as she took her shot. I laughed and then filled them in on the latest and greatest. By the time I was done, I was tired of speaking Lo's name.

"Don't even trip, Jae Money. When I see that hoe, I'm going to drag her ass just because I never liked her ass. The bitch is a bum and a thot."

I shook my head because I knew that Jamiya was serious. Nobody really liked Lo much after we started fooling around, they more so just tolerated her because of me and that was another reason I had kept my distance over the last couple of years. I didn't want anybody to have to be nice and have to fake like her ass. Lo was possessive, whiney and very self-centered, plus she was a party girl with a little bit of a reputation.

I mean, yeah, I knew that Lo had gotten around before but shit, I wasn't trying to wife her so it didn't mean nothing to me. She was just something to do while I was trying to cope with my grief, but now, sitting here talking to my family, I realized that I had been coping all wrong. I should have been running to my family for support and comfort and not away. I definitely owed everyone an apology and a whole a lot more than I had been giving. We grabbed the bottle and the tray of shot glasses and headed into the living room where the guys were with the kids.

I went and sat next to Dolo on the large charcoal grey sectional. I loved the décor in the family room. It was very contemporary and cozy. Tamia had helped China decorate her home and they did a great job together. The colors were charcoal grey and a deep plum color and it went so well. I looked around and smiled. I missed having my family around but I just wished that I had everybody with me. My son most importantly. Some days I woke up and cried until I fell back to sleep. I asked God over and over again why He would be so cruel and why was I the one that He chose to have everyone I loved snatched away from me. I didn't understand why He would allow me to endure so much pain and suffering.

"Got something on your mind?" I looked at Dolo and shrugged my shoulders. "Don't do that, sis. We family and we love you, so don't ever feel like you have nobody." I nodded my head and began pouring shots and handing them out. That was the reason Dolo and I were so close. He could read me like a book and his gangster ass always knew what to say.

We sat around clowning for a while and I noticed Q kept stealing glances at me. I hadn't really said much to him since he got here. I had mad love for Q. That nigga was most definitely the truth but I wasn't trying to make anything of it. He had a girlfriend and I would hate to have to beat Laniece's ass over her nigga. So yea, I was going to kick back and not even entertain them sexy glares that he kept giving me.

"Man, you drunks ain't hungry yet?" I said as I looked at my watch. "It's going on six and I'm starving." I stood up and grabbed baby Gioni from Gio's arms and kissed his cheeks as I went to place him in his bassinette in the room while China and Tamia headed to the kitchen to start making plates. It was funny how the baby was able to fall asleep in the middle of all that noise we were making. He was such a cutie and China said that he didn't cry much either, which is always great when it comes with babies.

After laying the baby down, I went to relieve my bladder. That alcohol was in me and had me full of it. I washed my hands and stared in the mirror for a moment. I needed some dick because I was starting to break out along my jawline and my rabbit couldn't clear that up. I smirked at the thought because I didn't even have anybody to give it up to. I mean, Sherrod was cool but that nigga was a hoe and I didn't really want to take him down. It was cool the few times we messed around and he gave me head but he wasn't really somebody I wanted to make a habit of. I needed a consistent cutty buddy, not just a one-night stand. I definitely didn't want a relationship, though. Like, not for a very long time.

I walked out the bathroom and I bumped right into Q. "Damn, nigga, the fuck you creeping around for, stalker!" I said as I pushed him in his chest.

He laughed and grabbed my arm. "You ain't going to keep putting your dirty ass hands on me, Jae. I'm not Lo. I will knock your little ass out. Fuck with me."

I laughed at his crazy ass. He was always talking shit but wouldn't do shit. "My nigga, please, you ain't trying to see me, though." I tried to pull away and walk off but he pushed me against the wall and took a step closer to me. I was now with my back against the wall and he was so close to me that my titties were pushed against his chest. My breathing became deep and heavy. I hadn't been this close to Q in a long time. We had a moment about a year ago where things got carried away and we took it further than either of us intended to but nobody knew about that episode.

That night with Q was just one time and we were both drunk as hell. We were in Vegas and Q was supposed to be driving me back to my hotel room where Lo was waiting on me. In the car, things got kind of touchy feely and we were real flirty with each other. One thing had led to another and I had his dick pulled out from his pants and was stroking it as he drove. Once we had pulled up to the hotel, he had gotten out to help me out of the car and I kind of just attacked him. I was all over him the moment my feet hit the pavement. We had sex on the hood of the car, drunk as hell at four in the morning in the parking lot of the hotel. I knew I was out of pocket because Lo was waiting for me and I was outside getting my back blown out by the nigga that I had been crushing on since before her and I were ever fucking around. I never regretted that night, though, and it was kind of special to me. Q was the full package and I was glad to have sampled that batch of greatness. That nigga was the prototype for real niggas.

I looked up and into Q's eyes as he stared at me intensely. "Why you always playing with a nigga? I think you really just like being smashed on, with your freaky ass," he said as he licked my neck. I put my head back against the wall and let him lick and kiss all up on me as he whispered in my ear. I knew I was tipsy because I didn't even have the desire to push him up off of me. He felt and smelled so good and it was just as intoxicating as the tequila that we were drinking.

I lifted my head and kissed him on his cheek. "Tuh, boy, please. You ain't never smashed on me. Who are you trying to fool?" I smirked and then kissed his lips.

He looked at me and we engaged in a deep kiss. Q slipped his tongue in my mouth and I allowed it to roam as I explored his mouth with my own tongue. I pulled away as the doorbell rang. I looked at Q and smirked, we were lip locked in the hallway and anybody could have walked up on us. I didn't really care but I'm sure it would have been the talk of the weekend so I was glad that we had stopped. I walked away and looked back at Q. I smiled as he winked at me while wiping his lips. I walked back into the kitchen at the same time as Q's girlfriend Laniece. I smirked at the situation then looked at her and gave her a head nod.

"Where is Quinton?" she said as she grabbed a wine cooler from the refrigerator.

I looked at Tamia as we locked eyes and she turned her nose up at how comfortable this bitch had just made herself. None of us really liked Laniece. She was stuck up and a real square. I hated having to rephrase shit when we were having conversations just so that she could understand. Laniece was originally from Seattle but had lived in Vegas since college. She was a graduate of UNLV and was boring as fuck to keep it simple. I mean, don't get me wrong. She was cute in the face and had a cool shape but she was basic as hell and wasn't necessarily my cup of tea. I chuckled because I knew Q heard his bitch walk in and his rude ass still hadn't come in here.

"Something funny, Jae?" she asked.

I turned on my heels and faced her. "Now Laniece, sweetie, you know I don't fuck with you like that for us to go by nicknames. Jaeda is just fine to say and it doesn't exert any extra energy." I gave her a fake smile and walked out of the kitchen. I didn't have time to be petty with her tired ass.

I walked into the living room and sat down on the ottoman in front of Greg and leaned back on his knees. The guys were having a heated discussion about which females from *Love and Hip Hop Atlanta* had fake asses. They were arguing and talking shit like these broads were their wives or something.

"Q, while you in here talking about ass and bitches that you haven't met, yo' bitch in the kitchen looking for you in the cabinets," I said as we all burst out laughing.

"Ha ha, very funny, nigga. I heard her in there. I was trying to let y'all bond a little," Q said as he mashed me in the side of the head with a pillow.

"Please, my nigga. Ain't no way I'm going to be sitting up in there bonding with her boring ass, because ain't shit popping about that hoe. So go get wifey before she get too comfortable," I said as I mashed his ass back.

"That ain't wifey! You know what it is," he said as he looked over his shoulder.

I smirked and pulled out my phone to take a few pictures with my niggas before I forgot. As we were taking pictures, China and Tamia walked in and started handing out plates. The food smelled good as hell and I couldn't wait to dig in. Laniece walked in with a plate in her hands and sat down taking bites from her food. I looked at Dolo and burst out laughing.

"Damn, Laniece, you must be hungry as shit," Dolo said as he continued laughing.

"Yes, that flight had me starving," she said, not even seeing her mistake.

"You know, if you were anywhere else, hoes would be jumping hurdles to bring your man a plate seeing that you didn't even bring him shit," I said, rolling my eyes at her simple ass. She definitely wasn't his speed. I would never sit down to eat and allow the next bitch to feed my man unless it's his mama and that still wouldn't be right because she would most definitely be talking about me once I left. Q's ass wasn't shit because he was just sitting there with a smirk on his face.

"It's smooth, Q. I got you little, bruh," China said as she and I walked back in the kitchen. I laughed as we walked back in the kitchen listening to China clown Laniece on the low. I grabbed two plates and started placing food on them. China had outdone herself with the food. She had made some jambalaya, fried and grilled garlic butter shrimp, garlic crab and fried catfish with some garlic bread and grilled salmon salad. I felt bad that I didn't come and help her put all this good eating together because it looked like she had slaved.

I walked back into the living room with both mine and Q's plates in my hands. Yeah, a bitch was being childish because I could have let China just bring it to him but I wanted Laniece to see how a real bitch did it and that if I wanted, I could swoop in on her nigga. I knew how to treat a king like a king but I knew this bitch had no clue. I handed Q his plate and winked at Laniece's basic ass as I copped a seat next to Rico.

"Aye B, why you ain't bring yo girl? I like her little pretty ass," Jamiya said as she stuffed a fork full of food in her mouth.

I snickered. "Yeah, I like her rude ass, too. That bitch came up in the club in Vegas tripping on hoes." We all laughed.

B had this girl that he had been seeing for the past eight months and she was cool as shit. Her name was Daisy and she was like five feet even, caramel complexioned and no more than 110 pounds but her ass did no playing. Daisy had met us in Vegas for fight weekend and when her and her girls walked in, she saw B surrounded by hoes. That little chick came through shoving bitches left and right until she was right up on B. When she got in his face, this bold ass hood rat tried to play tough like she didn't know what was up and Daisy ran up on that bitch and started serving breakfast. I liked her and she was definitely a good fit for my brother because she kept him in line and didn't allow him to be acting an ass out here making her look bad.

"Jae, you stay away from my bitch, with your gay ass!" B said with a straight face.

I laughed hard as hell. "Shut up, nigga. I don't want your bitch. I just had a lapse in judgment for a second," I said as I cracked open a crab leg.

Greg looked up at me with a smirk. "Bitch, two years don't count as a lapse in judgment. The fuck?"

We all laughed and I flipped him the bird. "Fuck y'all!"

We continued eating and drinking until the wee hours of the morning. I had really missed everybody being around each other and I was glad that we had all agreed to take this trip next week to Cabo. It would be a much needed get away for all of us and I was welcoming it with open arms. I lay on the floor of the living room as Rico lay across the couch. Dolo had left to go meet up with some girl and Q and his bitch went back to Q's spot. Jamiya and Tamia had just left and so had B and Greg. China was tired and with the help of the food and alcohol, she had been tapped out. But I couldn't blame her. She had a brand new baby, a hyperactive three year old and she had cooked all that good ass food. She deserved her beauty rest, but I was wide awake, just thinking.

Christmas was a couple of months away and I was probably going to spend it outside of the country. I didn't have my son here to shower with gifts and unlike the last two Christmases, I didn't want to lock myself in my house crying my eyes out.

"What you thinking about, Jae Money?" Rico asked as he kicked a pillow at me.

I paused for a second before I answered. "Life, brother. Life and how crazy and cruel it can be," I said as

I turned on my side facing him and put the pillow under my head.

Rico just stared at me but he didn't speak, so I closed my eyes and just relaxed. "I know I'm just coming home, sis, but you know you my nigga and there ain't nothing in this world that I wouldn't do for you. Shit, you held me down the whole time I was down and for that, you got my respect and love for life." I opened my eyes and looked at him. I had missed this nigga a lot. Letters and fifteen minute phone calls twice a week wasn't shit compared to having him right here in front of me. "Hear me, though. I know you still grieving. You lost a lot over these last few years but it's time to let your heart heal. You only damaging yourself more and more when you trying to coat pain with drugs and alcohol." I looked up at Rico and he was laying there with his eyes closed as he talked. "On some real shit, love and time have nothing to do with each other. There is no time limit on when you stop loving and caring for somebody once they aren't in your life anymore and there is no time limit on when you can start loving someone else after a heartbreak. If it's real, it will come right on time. So I'm here if you need me but don't block your heart because you're scared to hurt again. Life is a game of chances and everything we do there is a chance that we can get hurt again but there is also the chance that we can be happy. But we will never know unless we take that step. You feel me, though?"

I just stared at Rico with tears running along the side of my face. "Gotti, when you get so wise? You in here sounding like Iyanla and shit," I said as we both laughed.

"Man, sis, sitting down will do that to you. Have you seeing life from a whole another angle but not all niggas gain knowledge after jail. Shit, some come out just as stupid as they went in."

I smiled and closed my eyes, soaking in what Rico had said. I heard him loud and clear. "I love you, Gotti. Glad you back, nigga," I said, but his ass must have been half sleep because he responded with a half assed "Mhmm."

I was too tired to go into the guestroom, so I pulled up the covers and let sleep take over.

Chapter 7: Big Money Q

I sat back on the couch watching Big Donks #37. I was loaded and horny as hell but Laniece had gone to sleep on me. This routine was starting to get old. Her ass always played the tired role like she couldn't bust it open for a real nigga. She was already against giving head, so the least she could have done was stay up and let me get my dick wet for a good thirty minutes.

I picked up my phone and saw that I had a video message from my little bitch out in the City. Tia was this little dark chocolate bitch from Hunters Point in San Francisco. She was a hustler straight up and down. She didn't have a 9-5 and she didn't have any kids. Tia had been grinding in the Tenderloins since she was 17 and she had never really stopped. I mean, she had other hustles but that was the one thing that she never stopped. There were plenty of times that we had fallen off and I couldn't get in touch with her but I could always go to the TL's and catch her posted. I fucked with her tough and had been for a few years. She was 23 and was with the shit. I liked her because it wasn't any drama between us. She had a nigga but he had been down the whole time that we had been talking. Although she fucked around with me every once in a while, she held him down and made sure he wanted for nothing. He was due to come home in a few months after a 5 year bid so she had been hitting me up hella much to see me.

I looked at the video and let out a low whistle. Tia was bent over and she was clapping her ass and twerking in a sexy black stringy panty set. Her ass was looking so right. I took off my t-shirt and pulled my dick out of my shorts. I turned the TV down so that I could hear Laniece if she woke up. I didn't really think she was really going to wake up but I was just being cautious. She didn't much trip off of me watching porn but she would blow a gasket if she saw that the next bitch was sending me videos like this. I watched the video as I stroked myself. The shit was looking good but I needed the real thing. I had told her earlier that I wasn't going to be able to see her tonight like planned because my broad had come in town.

I stuffed my shit back into my shorts, threw my shirt back on and stood up to leave. I shot a text to Tia and told her to meet me at the Marriott in downtown Oakland. I grabbed my phone, keys and a hoodie and was out the door. I knew I was out of pocket but shit, I didn't understand why Laniece's dumb ass came and got on a plane, popped all up on a nigga and went to sleep without giving me some ass. Shit, if that was the case, her ass could have stayed at home and let me get some outside ass in peace. Now I knew when I came back to the spot, she was going to be acting a fool and I ain't feel like dealing with all of that. I pulled out of my driveway and headed toward the hotel. "Cut Her Off (Remix)" with Boosie came on my Pandora station and I chuckled at the irony. Shit, maybe it was a sign that I needed to cut Laniece's ass off.

Shit, I needed a bitch that knew how to treat me and that was attentive to my needs. All she was ever worried about was whether I was out here trying to fuck on Jaeda. Shit, you would think with all her worrying, she would attempt to make sure my dick never went dry. I rapped the words to Boosie's verse as I drove and tried to figure out when would be the best time to break it off. If it wasn't for this Cabo trip, I would probably do it when I came back home but her ticket had already been purchased. I could always still cut her off and then take someone else to Cabo but I really didn't want to bring no other bitches around. Tia wasn't my bitch and my eyes were on Jaeda, so I couldn't bring no females around, especially on a family trip and then expect for her to take me seriously when I came at her with this real shit.

***

I woke up the next morning and looked around as I heard the door to the room open and then close followed by the smell of food. Tia walked in with breakfast and I got up and went to the bathroom to take a leak and brush my teeth. Once I handled that, I walked back into the room as Tia was setting out the food on the small table. "I grabbed you some French toast, scrambled eggs, turkey bacon and a yogurt with some coffee, extra sugar," Tia said as I sat down rubbing my hands together.

I was glad that she wasn't the type of female that I had to tell everything to. She just did what I needed and got exactly what I liked and I didn't have to tell her what to do, she just was always on point. As a man, I had no problem treating my girl like a queen and catering to her. Yeah, I was a hood nigga but I knew how to take care of home, especially when home was taking care of me.

As I grabbed my things to leave, I thought about what it was that I wanted and honestly, it wasn't a thing or a list of things that I wanted. I wanted Jaeda. I had given her time to grieve and do her before really pushing up on her but a nigga was tired of waiting. I needed her bad and I couldn't let her get too free, feeling freshly single and let her go get with the next nigga or whoever. Shit, with Jaeda, who knew what would happen next.

I walked towards the door and Tia was throwing her items into her overnight bag. "You straight, T? You need anything?" I said as I pulled my wallet from my back pocket.

"I'm good, Big Money, you ain't got to tip me off like I'm a hoe or something, nigga. I stay telling you that shit."

I looked at her and laughed, "My nigga, anyway, I just be trying to make sure you don't need anything. Feel me?" I tossed her a couple hundred and told her to get her car detailed because her shit was looking like it needed it. She laughed and we said our goodbyes.

I pulled up to the house and sat there for a moment. I wasn't ready to even go in and deal with this bitch at the moment. I was really done with this whole relationship. Wasn't shit appealing about it. I mean, yeah, Laniece was cute, educated and had her own money but the bitch was dry and wasn't my speed. I didn't have to deal with nothing with her except her mouth but I mean, she wasn't no hoe, didn't have no baby daddies running around and she wasn't no begging female but it just wasn't there with her. I couldn't sit around and chop it up with her ass like I could Jaeda. I couldn't just chill and expect her to relate with shit on the streets. I didn't see a future and I couldn't see us building together. Yet she felt differently because she was always talking about purchasing a home together and joint bank accounts, marriage and life insurance type of shit.

I looked out of the window as Laniece came walking out of the house in a pair of ugly looking hammer pants. I just shook my head preparing for the battle. She tapped on the window like I wasn't sitting there staring right at her ass. I rolled down the window with a blank ass face. "Really, Quinton? So you just get up and leave in the middle of the night? You didn't say anything I just woke up and you weren't in the house. How rude is that?" she yelled at me with her hand on her hips.

I knew she was pissed and it was crazy because I didn't have any sympathy about it. "My bad. You were knocked out and Dolo hit me and needed me to drive him home, so I crashed over there," I lied as I grabbed the blunt that Tia had rolled for me while I was in the shower.

"You couldn't say anything? Not a note or a text just giving me a heads up? We're in a relationship, Quinton, and the things you do at times are disrespectful. I sure hope that Jaeda wasn't spending the night at DeLawrence's house, too," she said, shifting from one foot to the other.

"Quit calling Dolo by his government before he fucks you up and why you always worried about Jae? She ain't never did shit to you but you always got her name in your mouth, so fall back. If you so worried about another bitch being around your nigga then why you ain't never popping that pussy for me?" I asked, just finally putting it out there.

Laniece just stared at me before she responded, "Quinton, why do you always have to speak so vulgarly? We do not have to have sex all of the time. I would appreciate if you learned to be intimate in other ways and not just by having intercourse."

I stared at her blankly. "Girl, I ain't about to get blue balls just because you want to talk and knit. Go on with all that square ass shit. A nigga need to get right and you be playing and then have the nerve to want to know who I'm fucking. Not you, bih," I said, taking a deep pull from my blunt.

Laniece just stared at me before walking away. "Whatever, Quinton. I am not about to entertain your nonsense. Can you take me to the mall so that I can get some last minute things for this Cabo trip, please?"

I hit her with a head nod and rolled my window up before I pulled back off because I needed to go to the store real quick but I wasn't about to tell her shit. Laniece turned around quickly and I could tell she was yelling after me but I was already down the block. I laughed then turned my music back up as I hit my blunt.

Chapter 8: Dolo

I walked out onto the beach and stretched my arms high above my head. I shook my head and laughed at the situation I had just walked out of. It was our second night in Cabo and the shit was dope. We had rented the six bedroom, eight bathroom Casa La Laguna villa for five days and it was day two and I probably still hadn't seen the entire property. I had just walked off of the Pardiso Perduto compound and I was most definitely feeling like that nigga.

Last night we had gone out as a group to dinner and then drinks at Mandala. That's where my night got interesting. I was chilling at the bar when I saw this bad ass broad come stand close to me. I was on her from the beginning. I ain't even the type of nigga that chases bitches like that but she was pretty than a motherfucker so I was willing to see what was up.

The broad's name was Henah and she was a 24-year-old Eritrean from San Diego. She had come out to Cabo for a family reunion. I ended up buying her and her cousins a few drinks and we were chilling. After a while, they were telling me how they had their own villa and wanted me and a few of my friends to come back with them. I grabbed Rico and Greg and asked if they were trying to come back with me. Greg was acting like a pussy, talking about he was going back to the Villa but my nigga Gotti was with it. Henah was fine as hell and her cousins were cute but she had a few of them that didn't get as lucky in the looks department but I wasn't tripping because I was only looking at Henah and Rico had got up on her cousin Liya, so we could all just chill until it was time for me to dig up in them guts. Then I didn't care what the rest of them hoes did.

By the end of the night, all of them hoes was drunk. Henah and her sister ended up wanting to have a threesome and what kind of nigga would I be if I turned that kind of party down? The crazy thing is that I woke up in the middle of my sleep getting my dick sucked. I opened my eyes thinking it was Henah or her sister and to my surprise it was neither one of them. One of their ugly, thick ass cousins had brought her drunken ass in and just started topping a nigga off. I can't even lie, that shit was fire. I knew I was wrong but I ended up taking her ugly ass into the bathroom and bending that thick ass shit over, giving her the last drops of this dope dick. I was so in the moment that I didn't really even think about strapping up. She had a nigga so gone off of the head that I just dove right in. I shook my head as I thought about how I had fucked up. How in the hell did I strap up all three rounds with Henah and Jayah but not with her ass? She had got up smiling all big, looking like Bill Cosby had spit her ass out himself. She said she was on the pill, so I grabbed my shit took a quick shower and dipped on all of them hoes. Henah had my number and I knew she would use it.

I walked in the front door of our home for the next few days. It was still fairly early in the morning and the house was quiet for the most part. This was the first time that the whole crew was able to come out and vacation all together. The Villa consisted of six master suites with six bathrooms as well as two half baths, two large dining areas, an infinity pool and two separate staircases that led to the balconies from outside. The view was amazing and there was plenty of shit to do out here. I wasn't even tired anymore. I was trying to take advantage of the time we had so I walked into the kitchen and decided to make some breakfast for everybody.

Everybody was paired off in rooms and Jaeda and I ended up being the oddballs out so we decided to room together. I walked into the suite expecting her ass to be sleep but she was wide awake, sitting up writing. "What you up doing, square?" I asked as she looked up at me with red glossy eyes. I could tell she had been crying but I didn't want to pry, so I didn't mention it.

"Shit, I was writing Lex and Uncle Ken a letter. Can you mail them off when y'all get back?" she asked as she began stuffing them into envelopes.

"It's all good, Jae. Come help me make breakfast." I kicked my shoes off and walked back out of the suite.

Once in the kitchen, I grabbed eggs, shrimp, grits and catfish and began grabbing seasonings. The ladies had gone to the local market yesterday and grabbed groceries to last us the time that we were going to be here. For the most part, we really just agreed on getting mostly breakfast foods. It would be a waste to not use the nice ass kitchen that we had.

"So you dipped off with them drunk ass hoes last night and just now bringing your thot ass home, brother?" Jae said as she entered the kitchen and placed the apron around her body.

I laughed at her silly ass. "First off, nigga, you putting on that apron like you really about to come burn something. I said help me. Fuck, you trying to take over or something? I'm the chef today and second, I'm a grown ass man though, dawg. Ain't no curfew, bih." I swatted her with the dish towel as we laughed and started cleaning and peeling the shrimp. I told Jae all about my crazy night. I was so ready to get out of there that I had forgotten all about Rico but she told me had come back earlier than I had. He was Mister Hit It And Dip for real. I guess that's how I ended up fucking on three bitches, by sticking around longer than I should have.

I put a pot of water on and began shredding some cheese for the shrimp and grits. I looked up at Jae as she was telling me all about Q and Laniece turning up last night. I was laughing as she was describing Laniece's ugly cry. "I don't know what that bitch did, but Q was hot. He crushed that bitch phone and hella shit. All I know is that he said she was sneaky as fuck and he was cool off her." Jaeda shook her head, still laughing.

"Damn, I wonder what happened with my nigga. I wish he would kick that bitch to the curb. Shit, she fucking up my nigga image and shit," I said as I dipped the catfish in the batter and began placing them one by one into the large skillets.

"How is she fucking up his image? She ain't ugly or nothing. She just boring as fuck. She cool, other than that and all that insecure shit she be doing," Jae said, shrugging her shoulders. "The bitch is just plain and boring and her ass needs to loosen up. Shit, I'm tired of her uptight ass but she ain't making him look bad."

I looked at her and shook my head. "See, that's the issue. You hoes always looking at how a bitch looks. Q fucking with this square ass bitch will have all the square hoes thinking they have a chance with my nigga and then when we're out, we not going to have no action with the nasty hoes because now my nigga going to have this persona that he wifing all the square bitches." I shook my head wildly as Jaeda doubled over in laughter. See, bitches didn't understand that wifing bitches went beyond looks and money. I couldn't have my niggas out here fucking off my pussy chances because they wanted to wife slow bitches.

"Y'all are retarded as hell. You need to slow down before your dick fall off. Get you a nice wholesome girl and have some kids or something before you catch something."

I looked at Jaeda with a frown on my face. "Only thing I'm going to catch is a check so rest assured that I wrap it up every time, this morning don't count," I said as I grabbed plates and handed them to Jaeda as she started placing food on them.

"Wow, something smells great in here." I looked up as Jaeda rolled her eyes hearing Laniece's voice.

I turned around and looked at her as she came in and grabbed a bottled of water from the refrigerator. "Laniece, I heard you and my nigga fonkin'. Don't be coming out here and fucking up the vibe and shit with that bootsy shit you be on," I said just as Q walked in the kitchen.

"Damn, you niggas in here cooking shit up. Who the fuck y'all think y'all are?" Q said as he leaned on the counter. Laniece walked up to him and leaned in to kiss him but he sidestepped her with a straight face. Jaeda was messy as hell because she couldn't hold her laugh in and that in turn made me laugh out loud, too. I looked at Laniece's face and I could tell she was mad as hell and embarrassed, too. I don't know what had happened but my nigga was not fucking with her ass. "You niggas ain't got no sense," he said as he grabbed a plate and walked into the dining area.

One by one, everybody had come into the kitchen to grab their plate and we all sat down for breakfast in the dining room and discussed what we wanted to get into for the day.

Chapter 9: Jaeda

I sat by the pool with my shades on, soaking up the rays. I really wasn't trying to get any darker but that was close to impossible out here in this sun. Everybody else was out shopping except for me, Q and Dolo. Instead of shopping, we decided to go down to the pool to have a few drinks and chill.

Q had just started to tell us what had happened between him and Laniece the night before. "So I'm on the iPad checking my emails and shit, and I guess her ass must have been on Facebook earlier and had forgotten to log out. so all of a sudden, I see the little chat icon pop up and it's a nigga face and shit, so I'm not no insecure nigga that be checking her messages and shit but the nigga sent like four messages back to back. So I open it up and this nigga sending pictures and talking about how he can't wait to see her and hella shit." I looked over at Q as he continued to talk because I wanted to hear what was coming next. Laniece always acted so goody two-shoes. I had to hear what kind of shit she had going on. "So when the bitch comes out the bathroom, I'm like bruh, who the fuck is this *Bossnigga Jay* dude and her ass gets all stuck, talking about some damn, 'Who?'"

I shook my head and laughed because he was getting hyped as he started telling the story. I looked over at Dolo and he was laughing already. I swear he couldn't stand Laniece just as much as me.

"Man, so I grab the iPad and shove it in her face like, bitch don't play with me right now. I'm like, *'Bossnigga Jay* from West Oakland. The nigga that said it was nice seeing you and asked when you were coming back out to the Town. This nigga that's sending you pictures of him.'" Q shook his head and took a swig from his drink before he continued, "So then the bitch start talking about she met him while she was in the Town the last time she flew in and that was all. So now I'm just pissed that the bitch sat there and tried to play me like I'm some lame nigga. Like bitch, you ain't slick at all and you definitely can't play a playa so come again with the truth, bitch. So she still lying and I open up her inbox and this bitch in that shit talking to like three different niggas and they all from Oakland, so I'm like bitch, hold on. Your only ties to Oakland is me, so while you popping up on me every time I come out here, you was just using that as a cover up to come and do your dirt and that's why you popping up and shit. So in all actuality, her ass was probably leaving right behind me to come out here and popping up days later like she just got in. that's why it was never any calls or nothing before she came. The bitch is sneaky and I'm hella cool on her ass all the way."

I shook my head at what Q had just said. It was funny how the square bitches sometimes end up being some of the biggest hoes. We all just sat there for a moment not saying anything, but I was seriously wondering how Laniece felt like she was going to get out of this one. "So do you think she was fucking any of these niggas that she was talking to?" I asked as I sat up and reached for my drink.

"Man, I ain't got to think nothing. Two of the niggas she for sure was fucking on because they was talking about how her shit tasted and felt and shit, the bitch had the nerve to be telling them all of our business and shit. Nah, I can't respect no hoe ass shit like that. I'm not a saint but bitch, you need to be damn near angelic fucking with me."

I stared at Q for a moment and thought about his last statement. I don't know why, but it had made me feel some type of way. I wasn't anywhere near being an angel. In the last year or so, I had done some questionable things. I wouldn't say I was being a hoe but I damn sure wasn't being a good girl.

I laid back on my chair and placed my shades back over my eyes. It felt so perfect out here and I had initially planned to stay for another week but I had changed my mind and decided to go back home. My house was back to normal and although I loved being out of the way, I needed to go home and get focused on making something of myself. I let out a deep breath before I realized Q was talking again.

"I ain't mad, bruh. I was already about to cut the bitch loose but she just made me feel like I should have been did the shit. The bitch playing with the pussy when it come to me, talking about we can spend time without fucking. Duh, bitch, because your shit still loose from the last three niggas you bust it open for. The fuck! Thot ass bitch."

I laughed at Q because he was really hella mad and I was just so surprised that this bitch had the balls to be out here cheating on him in his own city. Like damn, I guess good girls do love bad boys.

***

I walked to the edge of the Jacuzzi and stuck my foot in the water to test the temperature. The water was perfect; not too hot, but just right. It was a nice night and I just wanted to be outside enjoying everything that Cabo had to offer. The night was warm and the skies were clear. This was our last night here and I just wanted to relax until it was time to go back to the madness that I called my life. I stepped into the Jacuzzi all the way and sat back with my glass of tequila as I looked out into the ocean. Earlier we had gone out to the beach and got on the jet skis. My hair had been through hell out here and I couldn't wait to hit the hair shop once I touched down in the Bay.

The day had been real calm and fun filled and I was sad that it was time to leave but I knew that I couldn't hide away out here forever. I needed to get home and get my life right. I had fucked up enough and now it was time to grow the hell up and get on my grown woman shit. I grabbed my glass and took a sip of my drink. The shit was real smooth as the warmth from the alcohol slid down my throat. I closed my eyes and thought about my nonexistent love life. I didn't want to go back home and end up dealing with another lame ass nigga or sleeping around with no random ass niggas, especially when these niggas were nasty and untrustworthy. Shit, these Oakland niggas were all fucking on everybody. The Town was so damn small that you would for sure be fucking behind somebody you knew because these niggas were for everybody. I wanted my own man that I knew was all about me and not into having hella bitches because that shit was played for real.

I was about to be 21 years old and although I was still young, I knew what it felt like to be really loved. Tone and I were very young when we met, fell in love and then conceived a child but in that short time, he was everything to me. The love that we shared was real and even after he passed away I felt it. I still do now but I now know that I can move on and there is somebody that is out there for me that will love me like I deserve. Tone set the tone for the next love of my life and I know that even though he had his flaws, he gave me his all, so anything less than that is not for me. I heard once that true love will never return to you void so I would patiently wait for all that was due to me.

My eyes popped open when I felt somebody walk up behind me. I didn't even have to turn around to know that it was Quinton. His presence was just that strong. I could always feel his energy. It was the craziest thing to me.

"What's up, Big Money Q?" I said as I turned to look at him. He dropped his towel and lowered himself into the Jacuzzi. I watched as his swim trunks stuck to his body the lower he went into the water and smiled. Q didn't have a gym member physique. He wasn't super toned but his body was nice. His caramel skin was golden from the sun and he may not have had a flat, toned six-pack but his little baller belly was cute to me. Q wasn't fat, his arms were strong and his muscles were very evident. I loved the way his t-shirts cuffed around his biceps and his large, strong hands. Jesus! This man was fine as hell. I needed to get my ass up out of this damn Jacuzzi, and fast.

"What your ass looking at, girl? You look like you ready to eat me alive or something," Q said, laughing.

I shook my head and took a large gulp of my drink. "Nigga, please. Ain't nobody thinking about doing anything to you," I said as I looked into his eyes. I should have kept my mouth closed because he started moving towards me. "Watch out, Quinton. Stay your ass over there," I said as I backed away in the warm water. I couldn't do this with his ass today. I hadn't dealt with him since the time we had sex in the parking garage of that hotel. I was already tipsy and I knew that if I stayed around him too much longer then I might not be able to resist doing something that I know I shouldn't.

Q shook his head as he advanced and was directly in front of me. I had nowhere to go now. His arms were on either side of me and he was so close up on me that his breath tickled my lips. I leaned back as much as I could, this needed not to happen. Laniece was still here and even though he had broken up with her and had been throwing her shade all day, it wouldn't be right for her to catch us like this.

"Q, Laniece is here. Nigga, move," I said, placing my hand on his chest and trying to back him away from me. I could feel my body heating up the closer he got to me and I knew that in a minute, I wouldn't give a damn about anybody and I would let my body do all the thinking.

"Fuck that bitch. You telling me to move behind a thot bitch that neither of us care about ain't going to make me do anything but come get what I really want," he said as he leaned in and kissed my lips.

I pulled away and stared into his eyes. "I'm not the backup bitch, Quinton. You can't come to me just because it's fuck her."

Q backed away from me and shook his head. "Jae, I got one thing to tell you and I swear I won't ever say this again because if you don't get it now then you never will." I looked up at Q because his face had gotten that serious. The sexy bedroom gaze had faded away and now his jaw was tight. "I'm not one of them lame ass niggas that you may be used to being around on the block. I'm not that bitch ass nigga Chris that you wasted your time with and last but not least, I'm not that bitch Lo that you played around with. This shit may be a game to some niggas but I'm not them. I'm a grown ass man and I know what I want and whether it is now or two years from now, if I want it, I will work for it. I step to you because you what I want but don't ever get it fucked up like I'm trying to run game on you or play you out ya' pussy because I can get pussy wherever, whenever. But let me know when you done being a little girl and you ready for a real man. I'm a real nigga through and through but I'm a grown ass man above all of that," Q said as he stepped back and lifted himself out of the water. I just stared at him as he grabbed his towel and drink and walked back into the house.

I shook my head and leaned back as I sank into the water. I grabbed my drink and gulped it all down. I didn't mean to piss Q off but I just didn't want to be played with. And he may think that I am immature because of some of the things that I say or do but he of all people knows how much I have been through and my heart can't take any more pain. I sat there for a little while longer before I finally decided to get up and go find Q. I really wanted him next to me and I couldn't deny it no matter what my brain was screaming at me because my heart and body were yearning for his touch. I grabbed my towel and glass and walked inside. Everybody else, with the exception of Dolo, Q, Laniece and I, had decided to go out for drinks and dancing. Dolo was entertaining his little friend Henah that he had met and Laniece was just trying her best to stick up under Q even though his ass had told her to leave him alone. Shit, he had even told her to pack her shit and go home but clearly the bitch couldn't catch a hint to save her life.

I walked into the living room in my bikini with my towel draped around my shoulders, I looked around and Dolo and Henah were in the game room playing pool. She was a pretty girl with cinnamon colored skin and hazel doe-shaped eyes. She had the silkiest, darkest hair and was thick in the hips but I would still say she was slim. I waved as she looked up at me and smiled. "You're cute, Jaeda, and you look refreshed after your dip in the water," she said as I smiled.

"Thanks, boo. Dolo, where Q ugly ass go?" I asked as I stood in the doorway. I could tell that Dolo was kind of feeling Henah even if he would never admit it.

Dolo turned towards me. "I think he went into the kitchen to make himself something to eat."

"Good looking," I said as I made my way towards the kitchen.

I stood in the doorway as I watched Q move around. He was warming up some food that we had gotten when we had gone out earlier. "So you mad at me or nah?" I asked.

He never looked at me but continued moving around the kitchen. "I don't get mad, baby girl. I'm straight," he said as he went into the refrigerator and grabbed some lemonade, pouring himself a large glass.

I walked up to him as he sat down and said grace over his food. "Are you going to share?" I asked as I grabbed his fork and placed a scallop into my mouth. I purposely wrapped my lips around the fork and pulled it out of my mouth slowly and seductively. I watched him watch me as I handed him his fork back and blew him a kiss. I knew I was playing a dangerous game with him, flirting and shit right here in the kitchen where Laniece could just so easily walk in and start some shit, but I didn't care at the moment. I was low-key drunk and I just wanted to be close to Q.

Q laughed and shook his head. "You better quit playing with me, Jae Money, before you get some shit started that you can't finish," he said.

We sat silently for the next few minutes watching each other as Q finished up his food. After he finished his food, I stood up and walked around to where he was and reached to grab his plate. Q was so close to my face that I leaned in and kissed his lips. I was never this aggressive but the tequila had me feeling myself and I was trying to feel Q's ass right now. He looked at me and stared for a moment before grabbing the plate out of my hands. Q then pushed my back into the island. He was so close up on me that I could feel his hard dick up against my stomach as he leaned down and kissed my lips. I knew that this was the wrong place, wrong time but it felt so right. I felt his hands as they found their way down to my pelvic area and began to rub around my clit. His hands were like magic to my body and I could feel sparks shooting through me as he massaged my pussy through the thin fabric of my wet bikini bottoms.

"Mmm," I moaned as I pulled Q closer into me. I needed him badly and I was ready to feel him inside me. "I want to fuck you, Q," I said as I pulled away and looked into his eyes.

"Then come on and let daddy fuck you, Jae," he said, lifting me up under my ass and carrying me into the bathroom off of the side of the kitchen.

Once we were in the bathroom, Q placed me on the sink and stood between my legs. I looked up at him and licked my lips as he dropped to his knees and pulled me by my thighs to the edge of the counter. I threw my head back as I felt his soft, warm lips touch the flesh between my legs but just that touch alone had my entire body on fire. Q began to devour me as he hummed the melody to J. Valentine's "She Worth The Trouble" into my soaking wet box.

"Fuck," I moaned out loud. This nigga was giving me the business and he was only using his tongue. Shit, I didn't even know his thug ass even knew how to sing. He had only gotten through the first verse before I began to squirt my juices in his mouth. Q didn't back down, though. He grabbed a hold of my pearl with his lips and began to suck it roughly as I had another orgasm right behind the first. I pushed Q's head back and closed my legs as I lay back lazily against the mirror.

"Nah, fuck that. Bring that ass here, Jae. Come give me some," Q said with a sexy smirk on his face as he pulled his manhood from his swim trunks and dipped the head in first.

"You killing me, Quinton," I said as he dove into my pussy.

Q was giving me hard, long strokes and I was taking them like a G but that nigga was very well-endowed. Shit, he was tearing my walls up. I began thrusting my hips back at him. We were so in sync that it was crazy. I hadn't had my body handled like this in a very long time and I definitely needed this. Q plunged into me and just sat there for a moment before I began rotating my hips. His manhood was swirling inside my honey pot like a long handled spoon as I rode the wave of ecstasy. I bit down on my lip as I felt my orgasm building up. I had never had so many orgasms back to back. I wanted to blame it on the fact that I hadn't had any dick in a long time but I knew better. Q was that nigga and he was doing his thing. Soon as my orgasm subsided, I lay slumped over his shoulders before he pulled me down from the counter top and placed me on my feet and bent me over the sink.

Q played with the opening of my vagina for a moment, rubbing the tip of his dick on my wet pussy. I knew he was about to really give it to me now, so I braced myself and arched my back as he dove in and started banging my shit out. Q was hitting it so hard that I couldn't even make a sound. I was just breathing hard as hell. He grabbed my hips and began to pound my shit like he was trying to win a race.

"Ugh!" he grunted as he gave me two hard thrusts and I could feel his dick contracting as he released his seed inside me. I fell over the sink and he fell over top of me. We stayed there for a minute trying to gather our bearings.

"Watch out, nigga," I said as I tried to raise him up off of me.

Once he moved, I grabbed two rags from the cabinet and made them both wet and soapy, handing him one and then cleaning myself. I looked up into the mirror and stared back at Q as he stared at me. He winked at me and I looked away as I placed my bikini bottoms back on and walked out of the bathroom leaving him standing there staring at himself. I had to get away from his ass before I ended up not ever wanting to leave his side. I walked up the stairs and as soon as I landed on the top step, I bumped right into Laniece.

"Have you seen Quinton?" she asked as I walked past her and towards the room that Dolo and I were sharing.

"Girl, do I look like I got a leash on that nigga? Ain't that yo' nigga, though?" I asked as I mugged her ass and kept it pushing. "Retarded ass bitch," I said as I walked into the room and gathered my belongings to hop in the shower. My pussy was throbbing but it was that good pain that you smiled at because you felt it with every movement. That nigga Q was that nigga, on my mama.

Chapter 10: Jaeda

I walked out of my last class for the day and was so relieved to be getting the hell off of campus, but I was starving so I called into Gypsy's and put in an order for a lemon chicken salad and salmon fettuccini. I couldn't wait to dig into my food and then take my ass to bed. I had an important meeting in the morning so I needed to be well-rested so that I could be on my A game for what I needed to do. We had gotten back from Cabo a little over two months ago and I had wasted no time in trying to do things the right way. I had plenty money saved and I was bringing in dough every day but at the end of the day, I wasn't trying to be in the streets doing this shit forever.

I had only started back hustling to make sure that my uncle was straight but shit, he had daughters that wanted to keep this shit going but me on the other hand, I wasn't used to ducking bullets and looking over my shoulder all the time. Niggas knew me in the streets as Jae Money because I knew how to make a dollar and flip that shit and make it look easy. My whip game was A1 and my Gas Squad niggas in the East and the West was with the shit but on paper, I was nothing. I was a college student with no businesses or assets due to the fact that most of my possessions weren't in my name for protection from the FEDs. Lately I had been thinking of starting my own businesses. I was more than halfway done with school to obtain my bachelor's in business but I was ready to get the ball rolling. I had too much time on my hands and I wasn't trying to get into any more trouble.

I walked out of the building with a smile on my face. I had just met with Mark, an old friend of Uncle Ken. He was an older dude that had a few businesses in a few different cities and he was also an investor. I had talked to my uncle not too long ago and told him that I wanted to open an after-hours diner and he'd put me in touch with Mark. During the meeting with him and one of his colleagues, I presented him with my business plan that I had drawn up with the help of one of my professors. After looking over it and making some suggestions, we had initiated a contract and would become business partners in opening the first diner which would be right on the outskirts of Oakland in the city of Emeryville.

The diner would only be open from 9pm to 3am Monday through Friday and would be open Saturday and Sunday 9am to noon and then again from 9pm to 3am. This would be for the late nighters that wanted real food and not fast food. There would be a strict menu with only a few specialty items and beverages. I didn't want a large menu but I wanted my spot to be known for certain dishes and it would be better for business to prepare in bulk. It would definitely reduce the customers' wait time and the prep time at the beginning of the day would remain scheduled and prompt. My diner was for the party crowd, the late night grinders, the pregnant women with cravings and the overnight work crews. I was so excited that I would be a business owner soon that I was restless. I called up Gio and told him the good news. I had so much to do but I was ready to get the ball rolling. I felt good because he had said that he was proud of me and although he wasn't my blood brother, I had been around him so long and all I wanted was to have the people that I loved to be able to be proud of me.

I had gotten home around 5:30 in the evening. After the meeting, I had done some important running around. It was Friday so I had to hit the hood and collect money and also make deposits and made sure that my Uncle Ken, Lex, Aunt Shae, and Tommy all had money on their books and were straight with packages and everything.

By the time I walked in the door, I was exhausted but I had promised Dolo that I would go out with him so that we could celebrate my new venture. Everybody else was busy so it would just be me, Dolo and Tamia. I looked at the clock on the cable box and figured I could get a cool nap in before it would be time for me to get up and get ready. I walked into the kitchen and pulled a few

Red Bull cans out of the pantry and placed them, along with a bottle of white Remy, in the freezer to chill while I was sleep.

I woke up to banging on my door. I looked at my phone and saw that it was half past eight. I rolled my eyes and pulled myself off of the couch as the knocking continued. Just as I got up, my phone began ringing. "Hold on! Shit," I yelled as I made my way to the door. I opened it to see Tamia standing on the other side of it with her overnight bag in her hand. "Damn, bitch. You banging on my shit like somebody was chasing your ass or something," I said as I let her in and walked back into the living room.

"Girl, bye. If they were, I was for sure caught. I called you like five times and you didn't answer then I figured your ugly ass was in here knocked out so I was trying to make sure you heard me. You act like I broke the bitch or something." I laughed because Tamia was rolling her eyes and snaking her neck like she had a real attitude. She could be so extra at times.

I tossed her a couple of packages of weed and told her to roll up. I was ready to start getting faded but I was about to hop in the shower first. "Aye, can you call Dolo and see what time he's getting here? I'm making that nigga drive and he don't even know it," I said, mimicking Rick Ross as I walked out of the room.

I stepped in my bedroom and grabbed my clothes for the night. I had decided on a pair of high waist denim jean shorts, a white tank top and a white, blue and yellow floral blazer with a pair of yellow Steve Madden platform heels. I was going for the cute sexy look. I grabbed a bright yellow panty and bra set and threw that on the bed as well then I grabbed my shower cap and placed it on my head as I turned on the shower water and waited for it to heat up.

I stepped out of the shower and rubbed lotion on my body from head to toe. I loved the way this Jimmy Choo fragrance smelled on my skin. I decided not to wear any makeup tonight aside from a nude lipstick. I had gotten my lashes and brows done yesterday so I was going for the natural look. I put my clothes on and looked at myself in the mirror. I was looking good and would be feeling better once I smoked and took a couple of shots. I unwrapped my hair and let it fall around my face. My hair had grown a lot and I had decided to continue just wearing my wrap. I had streaks of honey blonde in it and it had gotten thicker and longer in the last couple of months and I loved how healthy it was looking.

I walked into my living room and I could hear Dolo's voice. Tamia was in the guest bedroom getting dressed so he must have been on the phone. I looked at him and he had his face frowned up as he sat there listening to the person on the other side of the line. I was trying to eavesdrop but now he wasn't talking. I didn't know why I was trying to eavesdrop like he wasn't going to tell me anyway. I guess my nosey ass was just impatient and wanted to know before he told me. I grabbed the cocktail glasses from the cabinet along with the Remy and Red Bull out of the freezer and carried them into the living room.

I walked in just as Dolo was hanging up the phone. "What's your issue, nigga? Why you looking like somebody kicked your dog?" I asked as I grabbed the bottle and poured some into each glass and opened my Red Bull.

"Man, sis, I feel like they did. You won't believe the call I just got." I watched as Dolo shook his head and took a sip from his glass. I lit the weed and hit it. My heart was beating fast because my first thought was that something had happened with Q but I knew how close they were so if he was still sitting here talking then it was something else. "Remember the bitch I bust in Cabo?" he asked.

"Yeah, Henah, right? Y'all been talking still haven't you?" I asked.

He nodded his head yes and hit the weed. "Yeah but she just called and told me to lose her number because us talking would be disrespectful to my baby mama," he said as he blew smoke up towards the ceiling.

I looked up and furrowed my brows at his statement. "Umm and who in the hell is your baby mama?" I asked.

I turned around as Tamia walked in fully dressed and sat down. I passed her a glass and a Red Bull as Dolo passed her the weed. "Who got a baby mama?" she asked as she hit the weed. I looked at Dolo waiting for him to tell us what the hell he was talking about.

"Man, her ugly ass cousin Ney, bruh. Henah handed the bitch the phone and this bitch hop on talking about she's 7 ½ weeks pregnant and shit. I can't let this bitch have this damn baby. She ugly as shit and I can't be claiming a half gorilla, half duck as the mother of my child. Fuck, this is so fucked up on so many different levels and Henah went bad like damn, nigga, you fucked my cousin. You already know I don't be worried about these hoes at all but damn, this shit making me look bad."

I shook my head and started laughing. I knew he was pissed but the situation was funny as hell. Dolo was a straight slut and he always was talking about bad bitches with fat asses and somehow karma had come around and bit him in the ass with this one. He had been dogging bitches for so long and now look. I would put my money on it that he would end up with a daughter, too.

Chapter 11: Jaeda

We walked into the club and I looked around. It was low-key cranking tonight. I stood off to the side looking on social media as I waited for Dolo to finish getting our VIP area taken care of. A cute brown skinned hostess walked over and directed us to our section. I looked around as I took my seat and saw a few familiar faces and it was like everybody was out to be seen tonight.

"Shit," I said when I realized I had left my blunt in the truck. I looked up as the hostess assured us that our bottles were on the way. We had gotten two bottles of Patron and a bottle of Rosé. I fucked with bubbly some but it seemed like now it started to give me headaches so I didn't want to overdo it.

"Sis, it's thick as fuck up in this bitch tonight. You good?" Dolo asked.

I looked over at Tamia and she was popping her ass in her seat. I nodded my head. "Yeah, I'm straight.

Let's turn the fuck up," I said just as the waitress came over and brought our bottles. Her and a sexy ass light skinned guy walked over and began to set up our table with glasses, ice and chasers. As soon as they walked away, we began popping bottles and trying to get even more faded than we already were.

We turned up together in our section watching everybody else as well. The club was turnt and the vibe was real as fuck. I pulled myself up and sat on the back of the couch and threw my hand in the air with the other hand holding my drink cup. It felt good to be clear minded and not off of drugs just to have fun and feel good. I was back to just weed and alcohol but I had even cut back on that a lot. I was feeling better than I had in a very long time. I had my days but for the most part, I was straight. My body had been tired and I stayed in the house for about a week just to rest and get my mind and body right.

I began nodding my head to Drake's "Back to Back" single. I wasn't a real Drake fan but that was a cool track even if it was a diss to my nigga Meek Mill. Tamia stood up and grabbed me and practically started dragging me out of our section and onto the dance floor. She had got juiced because the beat to Future's "Where Ya At" started playing behind Drake's song. I looked at Dolo and he looked like he had his eye on something. He nodded his head saying he was good and I followed Tamia out to the dance floor. Tamia loved to party but always had hella shit going on to where she didn't do it as much. I was happy she had come out to celebrate with me because we hadn't been out in a while.

We stepped on the floor and I watched Tamia go crazy as she started dancing to the song as the beat finally dropped. I was swaying back and forth with my cup in my hand. I was loaded and I had a big smile on my face as Tamia was leaned into my face rapping the words to the song, and I began rapping them right back at her ass. She was cute in an all-white body suit that clung to her thick thighs and exposed her cleavage and dipped all the way down her flat stomach, showing her silver belly ring. Tamia had a bomb ass shape. She was a little heavier than me but it was set in all of the right places. Her hair was styled into a cute blonde bob that was thick at the top and fell over to the left side of her face.

Tamia and I were having hella fun and were turned the fuck up. We had our cups in the air and I was doing a wobbly two-step as Tamia was bent over in front of me bouncing her ass to Migos. My cup went flying out of my hand as some bitch bumped me hella hard from the back. I bumped all into Tamia's ass and she had to put her hand on the floor in order to not fall over.

"Damn, bitch, you drunk?" she said as she turned around, looking at me.

"Hell nah, this dumb ass bitch just bumped me hella hard," I said as I turned around and put my hand on the back of the girl in front of me as she bucked back like she was trying to go dumb on me. The girl turned around as I gave her a little shove to put some distance between us. I was heated because I could tell she was purposely doing it because the song wasn't even as hype as she was.

"Bitch, keep ya hands to ya self," she said as she swatted my hand away.

I took a step towards her as I mugged her and gave her a quick look over. She was a little taller than me but I was ready for whatever. Tamia came closer to me and we were standing side by side as the girl eyed us like she was ready to get some shit popping. "Bitch!" I said with extra emphasis. "When you step into my space and bump into me, you lost ya rights to tell me where my hands can and cannot go. Shit, you lucky I'm not already beating your ass. The fuck!" I yelled, stepping closer to the broad. She was an alright looking bitch with some bald ass edges and beauty supply packaged weave. I shook my head. The bitch wasn't even worth the energy.

She stepped back and nodded her head. "Whatever, bitch. Think you hard and see where that gets you," she said as she winked her eye at me and walked off deeper into the crowd.

Tamia and I turned around and made our way back to our VIP section where Dolo was standing off to the side talking to a broad that was in the section next to us. She was cheesing hella hard and looked like she was ready to bust it wide open right here in the club.

I grabbed another glass and poured some Patron into it and took it down just as fast. It didn't even burn anymore. I was low-key drunk and I knew it was probably time we called it a night. I looked around and saw a familiar face. I sat back and watched for a moment because I wanted to see who they were with. I heard a loud crash to the right of me and turned my head to see what happened. I looked over and the girl that Dolo was just talking to had fell flat on her ass but had taken a couple of bottles down with her. I saw her friends standing there with annoyed expressions on their faces as Dolo helped her to her feet, which told me that this probably was a normal routine for her. I snickered a little and turned my eyes back to where they originally were focused on but I had lost the person I was watching. I looked all over the club but I didn't see them anymore. I was kind of mad that they may have already left or even more so spotted me and was waiting in the cut somewhere. "Damnit," I said as Dolo and Tamia walked over to me.

"You ready to cut?" Tamia asked.

"Yeah, let's go," I said and got up as I downed the last of the Rosé.

Dolo reached in his pocket and placed a hundred dollar bill under the bucket that the ice was in and we left. As we walked out, Dolo grabbed the waitress and let her know that he had left her a tip at the table. She nodded her head and then made a beeline for the table. We walked outside and the cold breeze hit me hard. I shivered a bit and then shook it off. I looked around and there were a few groups of people standing around as they had also left the club.

"Dolo, you got your shit with you?" I asked as I looked over my shoulder.

He fell back a couple of steps and then looked at me. "Yeah, I stay with it. Both y'all strapped, right?" he asked as we both shook our heads.

"We left ours in the car. Aye, so I just saw the nigga Tay in the club. You know, Richmond Tay that killed Laela," I said as I walked on the inside of the sidewalk so that I could keep my eyes on the individual on the other side of the street. "The nigga in the all-white right there was just with him in the club. Tay just dipped back on the back street to pee so when they get close to their car, I want to get on them and make it quick," I said as I watched Tay catch up to his patna.

Both guys had their phones glued to their ears so I knew they weren't on point. It's crazy how niggas do so much wrong in the streets and think it's safe to walk around like they're square. These niggas hadn't looked behind them or around them not once. It was cool because I welcomed their ignorance.

We walked up to Dolo's truck and all climbed in. Dolo had Tamia hopped into the driver's seat as he and I both hopped into the backseat of his truck. I pulled my hammer from under the seat and made sure it was loaded and ready. Dolo did the same thing while Tamia had started the truck and killed the lights. I watched as Tay and his friend had turned into the next alley and that was definitely an advantage.

I kicked off my heels and hurriedly threw on the pair of Jordans that I had brought along just in case anything popped off. "Tamia, keep the lights off, pull up to the corner and we're going to hop out. Once we get out, drive to the other end of the alley and wait for us. Keep your eyes open to make sure nobody is around," I said as I cocked my pistol and looked at Dolo. "You ready, nigga?" I asked. I don't know when the last time Dolo had gotten down but I knew that he was a certified shooter and I needed him to come out of retirement tonight and kick in.

Soon as the truck came to a stop, Dolo and I both jumped out of the truck and ducked down behind a car as we watched Tay get into the passenger seat. The two men sat there and hadn't even started the car yet. Tamia drove down the alley and passed the duo. Even from where I was crouched, I could see that neither of the men had even looked up as Tamia had passed them. Their mistake. I looked at Dolo and nodded my head. We stayed low and ran up on the car. We didn't have much time to go off of so we just started dumping. The first shot shattered Tay's window but the next three shots were all headshots. I watched as both men's heads exploded almost simultaneously.

"Go!" I yelled at Dolo as I reached in and grabbed the lighter that was on that nigga's lap, I pulled a stack of napkins and lit it on fire as I opened the gas tank and stuffed them inside, flame first.

I took off running and hopped in the truck and we took off, headed towards the bridge. I wiped my gun off as we got off at the Treasure Island exit. Dolo and I hopped out of the car as we pulled up by the rocks overlooking the water. I grabbed his hand and interlocked my fingers in his as we passed by couples that were out there trying to be on some drunken romantic shit. I was scared shitless because there were so many raccoons just out running around. We walked up on the rocks and Dolo leaned down as he grabbed the hoodie that was under his arm and tossed it into the water. Once we had tossed our weapons, we walked back to the truck and climbed in.

"Go to Denny's," I said as I stretched across the backseat and closed my eyes. I had just caught another body but I could breathe easier knowing that the nigga that took my family's lives was finally gone.

Chapter 12: Loren

"Damn, baby, that was some good shit. When you coming through again?" I asked as I checked my phone to see what time it was. I was supposed to be getting ready to go out with my girls later on but Diontay had popped up at my house and I wasn't about to turn down that good ass shit that he was slinging. I swear he could get a few years with the type of dope he was pushing, that dick was the truth.

"When I come through, bruh. Damn, quit acting like this some new shit. You know what it is. When I ain't getting that shit from wifey like I need it, I slide through here and you should be happy that I let you be second in command. I been coming through more anyway. Now come give daddy kiss and I'll get at you, ma."

I shook my head as I watched Diontay walk out of my front door. This was normal and I knew the only reason he had been coming over more was because him and his bitch were fonkin'. He wasn't my nigga but I had met him a few months ago on some high shit and ended up fucking him in the bathroom in the mall where we had bumped into each other.

I was the type of bitch that just did what I wanted and what I felt, whenever and wherever. So bitches would probably call me all kinds of hoes and thots for fucking a stranger in a public bathroom but I could give two fucks. Life was short and I was living. Diontay and I had met before Jaeda and I had even broken up and I had been fucking him on the regular behind her back. I loved Jae and all but she was spoiled and did what she wanted to do, so I never felt bad about creeping off behind her back. I knew he had a bitch and it was cool with me, at least at first, but now I wasn't feeling that shit. I had lost my bitch so it was time that nigga lost his. I was falling for Diontay fast and I wanted him to only want and need me. I was the type of bitch that he needed, not the square ass bitch that he was claiming as his wifey.

I refused to be a second choice to him. Especially now that I knew I was carrying his baby, I was about 17 weeks. From day one, he and I had never used any protection. I had told him that I was on birth control but honestly, I hadn't taken a pill in over a year. The moment I saw Diontay, I knew that I wanted him for good, so I was preparing to have my way. I hadn't told him that I was pregnant yet, though, because I was waiting for the right moment. I had been keeping this secret for the past three weeks. I really was scared of what he would say. I knew that he loved his bitch but I was trying to be the one he chose and not just because I was pregnant. I also was using this time to give him a little extra push at breaking up with his bitch.

Soon as he walked out of the door, I grabbed my phone and sent the pictures that I took of him while we were fucking to his bitch through my fake Facebook page. I never said anything to her, I just always sent pictures of when we were together. I made sure that I only got shots of his naked body and there was no background or anything. She would always send back to back messages but I would never respond. I had like six fake pages so that I could rotate back and forth, I had this bitch thinking that he was fucking hella different bitches daily. I had been sending messages for the past two weeks and that was why they were currently at odds. That's how I also knew that Diontay was fucking more than just me and her because he hadn't even asked if I was the one behind the messages. I played my part well so I knew it would be a while before he caught on. I kept him high off the best weed, kept his stomach full and most importantly, his nuts were always empty when he left. I was his confidant when he wanted to vent about the streets or his bitch and even about his crack head ass mama.

Once I had sent the pictures, I walked into my bathroom and turned on the water. I waited for it to get hot and then stepped in. I loved my water steaming hot. I lathered my wash rag and began scrubbing my body. I smiled to myself as I noticed the small baby bump that I had. I was barely showing and I was glad because I wasn't ready to tell anybody yet but I was excited to be carrying Diontay's baby. I knew that no matter what, my baby and I would be set. Diontay was a hustler and he was getting his paper. Plus, his daddy was an ex-football player for the Oakland Raiders so he had more than set him up to make sure that he was good. I could tell that he had money the day we met. I was a nasty bitch but I wasn't stupid. This pussy didn't pop for a broke nigga and my tongue was addicted to money. Shit, Jaeda's ass was paid out the ass so that night in Miami, I had to taste her. I knew she had some bread but I didn't know just how papered up she was until we took that trip to Miami and I happened to glance at her laptop and see her bank statement. Once I saw that, I knew I had to have that bitch. My sex game was top shelf and I knew I possessed the power to turn a bitch out and make a nigga crazy. So since Jaeda was obviously on bullshit then I was moving on. Diontay was about to have to deal with me for the next 18 plus years. It wasn't going to be as easy to get rid of me.

I twirled in the mirror and checked myself out. I had on an all-black mini t-shirt dress paired with some red snakeskin tie up heels and a matching red snakeskin headband. I added MAC's Ruby Woo lipstick and a little blush and eye shadow and I was set to go. I grabbed my wristlet and locked my doors on the way out and headed to my girl Rhea's house so that we could hit the club. I reached into my bra and grabbed the E pill that I had and popped it into my mouth. My face automatically scrunched up from the taste of it but I swallowed it dry and started my car and pulled out of my parking stall and into traffic. I knew that I shouldn't have been drinking and taking drugs along with going out but it was still early and I figured it wouldn't do much harm.

I pulled up to the curb and placed my car in park. "Bitch, come on!" I yelled into the phone at Rhea.

I looked up and Rhea and her cousin Dea'ra were both coming outside. I fucked with Dea'ra. She was real cool and she liked to party, too. She was a student at UCSF and we had messed around a couple of times, mostly just on drunk nights after we had gone out or something but not on a sober tip. The two of them hopped in the car and I took off headed across the bridge.

"Here, bitch, you drinking or nah?" Dea'ra asked as she passed me a water bottle filled with what smelled like Pineapple Ciroc.

I grabbed the bottle and took a couple of swigs as I passed a blunt and a lighter to Rhea so that she could fire up. We continued to get faded the entire drive to the club and by the time we had pulled up, I was feeling nice. I was ready to twerk something and hopefully Diontay would be calling me so that we could end our night together but if not, then I wasn't above finding a replacement. I was horny 95% of the time so I always needed to have somebody that could come and cool this kitty down.

The three of us stepped out of the car and headed towards the club. The line wasn't too bad right now so we shouldn't be in line for too long. I eyed the bitches that were standing in line in front of us and the ratchets were definitely out in full effect. I turned my nose up at this short light skinned nigga that kept staring at me from the front of the line. He was about 5'5" with gold tops and he just wasn't that nigga. I adjusted my body to where my back was to him and started making small talk with my girls. We were talking about the latest celebrity drama when Rhea told me that the light skinned guy was coming towards us. I rolled my eyes up into my head.

"'Scuse me, ma, you sexy as fuck. How about y'all come inside with me and my niggas and come chill in our VIP?" he asked.

I turned and faced him with a half-smile on my face. I figured I could entertain him for the night just so that we could be comfortable in the club. "That's cool with us, what's your name?" I asked him as I licked my lips for good measure.

"My name Danny, and them my niggas Terry and Jacob over there. What's your name, ma? I thought you were going to turn me down the way your mean ass was over there mean mugging me a second ago," he said.

"I'm Loren and these are my cousins Dea'ra and Rhea," I said as we followed them up to the front of the line where we were given wristbands and ushered inside.

I looked around as we walked in and saw that the club was packed. We walked across the main floor to one of the lower sections. I did a double take as we passed by the hostess' desk and I smirked as I passed Jaeda and her cousin Tamia. They were so engrossed in their phones that neither of them had seen me. "Stupid bitch," I said under my breath. I couldn't front, though. She was looking good as fuck in them short ass shorts. Her heels had her legs looking right and I wanted to really just drop down and lick that shit for old time sake but just as much as I wanted to taste her, I wanted to slap the fuck out of her ass. I hated her but loved her at the same fucking time. But at the end of the day, I knew that ship had sailed. I was looking forward to a future with my baby's father and I wasn't losing that battle. We stepped in our section and Rhea and I sat down on the leather sectional as Dea'ra had walked over to Jacob and started bouncing her ass in his lap. We had all met in the strip club so none of us were the shy silent type. They were just like me. If we wanted it, then we went for it, no holds barred.

Once the bottles arrived, we wasted no time popping them open and getting the party going. I handed both Rhea and Dea'ra a pill and I popped a second one. The three of us grabbed our cups and held them in the air for a silent toast and downed our liquor. The guys joined in on the next round and we went round for round with them until they started playing "Planes" by Jeremih. That was my shit so I got my ass up and started doing a slow wind, dropping my ass real nice and slow in front of Rhea as she ran her hands through my hair while licking her lips at me. I brought my body back up as J. Cole's verse came on and was snatched by my waist. I turned around facing Danny and I gave him a seductive lap dance as he rapped the music to me. Danny wasn't my type but he and his crew would do for entertainment, at least until something better caught my eye. I most definitely wasn't trying to leave with him but as I started grinding my ass on his lap, I felt him harden beneath me and I could tell he had a big dick. "Mmm," I moaned. Shit, if all else failed, I would run him in the parking lot but I wasn't going home with him.

Once the song was over, Dea'ra suggested that we go hit the dance floor and mingle. I was with it so we refilled our glasses and headed to the dance floor. I looked back and winked at Danny as I walked away seductively and swayed my hips to the music that was blasting through the speakers. Once on the dance floor, we walked up to the bar and I noticed Jaeda and Tamia coming down the stairs from the top VIP sections. I grabbed Dea'ra and pulled her into me so that I could talk directly into her ear.

"Damn, bitch, what's the secret? You fucking up my high," she said as I threw my arm around her shoulders.

"Girl, bye. Look, there go my ex Jaeda right there. That bitch going to play with my emotions and she just out living it up carefree like I never existed. I should go slap that bitch!" I said angrily. Dea'ra raised her index finger and walked off, leaving me standing by the bar.

I watched as Dea'ra grabbed Rhea's hand and they walked over to where Jaeda was dancing with her cousin. She didn't know Rhea or Dea'ra so she would never even know what was going on. I smiled to myself as I watched them start dancing next to Jaeda. They were playing Migos "Fight Night" and all of a sudden, Dea'ra started going stupid all on Jaeda. She was bumping all into her and hella shit. Jaeda bumped into Tamia and almost made her fall. I covered my mouth as I watched on in amusement. Jaeda and Tamia had turned around and looked as if they were ready to start thumping. Both sets of girls were exchanging words and while Jaeda and Tamia looked heated, Rhea and Dea'ra looked more amused. I watched on as Rhea and Dea'ra walked back towards me. I turned my back to them so that Jaeda wouldn't see me.

Just as they approached me, I looked up and spotted Diontay and Quise, his right-hand man, standing on the other side of the bar with some bitches all in their faces. I was pissed. This nigga said that he had some shit to handle tonight and didn't know when he would be through but lo and behold, here he was, standing in the club whispering all in the next bitch ear.

I walked over to where Diontay was standing and leaned in to him. "What's up, baby?" I said as I kissed him on the cheek. He and the bitch he was talking to both looked at me with surprised looks.

"Lo, why you got your ass all in the club with that short ass shit on? You done came over here fucking up my motherfuckin' vibe, though," he said as he stepped towards me with a mean mug on his face.

The girl stepped up as well. "Who is this, boo?" she asked while trying to loop her arm in his. He quickly dropped his arm so that her arm fell to her side. I smirked because the bitch needed to fall back before she really played herself.

"Aye how about you kick back and let me have a moment," Diontay said as he looked at the duck looking bitch standing next to him. She smacked her lips but still didn't budge.

"Damn bitch get a clue, my nigga said fall back." I said as I stepped towards her. After looking me up and down, she got the point and walked off to the bar.

Diontay turned his attention back to me and leaned in so that he could whisper in my ear. "Take your ass home and get that pussy ready for daddy. This ain't the place for you to be," he said. I knew he was just trying to get me out of his business but I nodded my head anyway. He kissed me on the lips and patted me on my ass as he headed towards the dance floor. I grabbed my girls and told them I was ready to go.

We headed back to our section and those niggas were up in there looking corny as hell. They had about five random bitches up in there doing all kinds of shit. One of the girls had her hands in Danny's pants jerking him off. I scrunched up my nose and grabbed the bottle of Belaire Rosé off of the table and poured it down my throat before I turned around and walked off. "This could have been you, Loren!" I heard Danny yell as I walked off. I flipped him off. He wished. I would never play myself like that in the club behind a nigga that couldn't even pop bottles with my ex bitch.

Soon as we got outside of the club, I noticed that Diontay and Quise had also walked out. They were with the same bitches that I had just walked up on. I shook my head as I kicked back a little and watched them from a distance. Diontay and the duck bitch stood talking for a minute and her thirsty ass was all over him, rubbing her hands all over his arms. He wasn't really doing anything back to her but he wasn't shutting her down, either. Diontay grabbed her phone and put his number in. the girl leaned in and tried to kiss him but he leaned to the side and the kiss landed on his cheek. They went their separate ways and then so did me and my girls. I watched the direction that Diontay went in and watched as he and Quise both walked to the car. Rhea, Dea'ra and I walked to our car as well.

Once we got in the car, I looked down at my ringing phone and noticed that Diontay was calling me. We made plans to meet up at the Denny's in Emeryville before we went back to the house. I was starving so I let him know that I would see him in a minute.

We got seated in Denny's and ordered waters as we waited for the guys to arrive. I looked at my phone wondering where the hell these niggas were at. I had called his phone over and over and it was going straight to voicemail. I figured he was just faking so we ended up ordering our food to go. I was tired of sitting in here and all the different smells were making me feel sick. Soon as our food arrived, we got up and exited the restaurant. Walking through the parking lot, I started calling Diontay's phone one last time as I bumped into somebody. I looked up and was face to face with Jaeda.

"What's up, bitch? I see you've been hiding real good, hoe, but I for sure got an ass whooping with your name on it." She said.

I looked at her and backed up a little. I know I talked all that shit about what I wanted to do to her but I really wasn't in the mood to be fighting her ass tonight. I tried to walk past her and she grabbed my arm. "Jae, ain't nobody got time to be fighting you. It's almost three in the morning. A bitch drunk and tired. Go on with that shit," I said and no sooner had the words left my mouth, she had punched me in my mouth.

I tried to block her blows but she was raining them down on me fast, I was too high to keep up with her. I pulled my blade from my bra strap and swung at her. I was in so much pain and I really was just trying to back her up off of me so I just kept swinging at her. I watched as her body dropped to the ground and blood was soaking her clothes. I covered my mouth with my hands.

There was so much blood but I knew I had to get the hell up out of there before Dolo or Tamia came out and saw me. Rhea and Dea'ra were already waiting in the car, where Jaeda and I were, we were hidden from where too many could have seen us. I ran to my car and jumped in. My heart was beating so fast that I could hear it in my ears. I didn't know how much damage I had caused but I knew that I had to get the fuck up out of dodge.

Rhea and Dea'ra kept asking me a million questions but I didn't say a word. I rode all the way home in complete silence until I dropped them off. Once I got home, I let out a deep breath. The whole way home, I kept looking in my rearview mirror thinking that the cops were going to get behind me and pull me over any minute. I was a big ball of nerves and I just needed something to calm my nerves. "Where the fuck is Diontay?" I said out loud as I walked to my bedroom.

I opened my top drawer and pulled out a baggy from up under my underwear. I held the baggy up and smiled to myself. I was trying to calm down on how hard I was partying because I was pregnant but right now I needed something to calm me down. I emptied the baggy on my nightstand and pulled my bank card and a twenty dollar bill from out of my wristlet that I still had around my wrist. I made four separate lines and rolled up the bill. My palms were sweating just from looking at the white powdery substance. I leaned down and snorted two lines back to back. It had been a few weeks since the last time I had snorted some powder and the feeling I was getting was just what I needed.

I lay back on the bed and just enjoyed the feeling it was giving me. After a couple of minutes, my heart rate had returned to normal so I sat up and attempted to call Diontay for the last time. Once again, his phone had gone to voicemail so I left a message. His ass probably decided to go home to his bitch. I was past the mood of having company now, so I turned on Meek Mill's *Dreams Worth More Than Money* album and decided to clean my house. It was after three in the morning and I had lost my appetite and everything else, so I scrubbed my house from top to bottom until I passed out.

I woke up the next morning sprawled out across my bed. I still had on the rubber gloves that I had used to clean out the refrigerator with. I shook my head as I sat up and looked at the time. It was only a quarter past 8 in the morning and I remember 5:15 was the last time I had seen on the clock while I was cleaning.

I got up and stripped down to my birthday suit. My music was still playing so I turned on Pandora and turned to Chris Brown's station before I got into the shower. I thought back to last night and got pissed off that Diontay had shook me and didn't even have enough respect to hit me and say shit. I wondered how Jaeda was. I really wasn't trying to hurt her but I kind of just blacked out.

When it came down to it, I had a real soft spot for that bitch even though she had played me and didn't feel for me like I had felt for her but when it came down to it, she had a good heart and I knew once she had finally seen me, she was going to try and beat my ass. I had left her house and fucked it up along with her cars and I had stolen from her. Now that I thought about it, I had really fucked up. I started to get nervous thinking about what Jaeda's family was going to do to me if Jaeda did pull through. I knew for a fact she would tell them what I did.

If they started looking for me, they had the connections to get to me as long as I was in the Bay Area.

"Fuck! What am I going to do now?" I asked myself out loud. I slid down to the floor of my shower and sat there as the water cascaded over my body. I could never just do something right in my life. I had a baby daddy that already had a bitch at home, I was fighting to keep my contract with H&M and I had just stabbed my ex-girlfriend.

I sat on the floor of my shower and cried for what felt like hours, but was more like thirty minutes. I just wanted to be loved and appreciated for what I was. I knew that I wasn't an angel but I knew that God had made somebody for me. I knew plenty of promiscuous girls that had found love. They say you can't turn a hoe into a housewife but I knew plenty hoes that were doing damn good as housewives. I didn't care what nobody said. My pussy was still tight and sweet. I may have gotten around a little but the product was still good. I just wished that Diontay would see me for what I was worth and that was a good fucking woman.

I pulled myself together and stepped out of the shower. I was out of energy. This pregnancy and partying too hard was taking its toll on me. It was a Sunday morning and I just wanted to stay in bed all day. I didn't want to go anywhere or see anybody and I didn't want to do a damn thing but stuff my face and get some shut eye. I threw myself back on my bed butt naked and just lay there staring at my ceiling. After a couple of minutes, I decided to go through my pictures from last night and post some on my Instagram. I had taken about thirty pictures but I only liked two. I deleted the rest and posted the two on my page. I began to browse through my timeline. It was a shame how every other day there were RIP posts all over my newsfeed. I scrolled through my timeline and ran across a picture that caught my eye so I tapped on the page and went to the picture. I looked at the picture and my mouth dropped open in shock. I just stared at my phone for a minute because I couldn't believe what I was looking at.

Tears just dropped from my eyes instantaneously. My heart was pounding so hard I could hear it in my ears. I shook my head as I exited from Instagram and logged into my Facebook. I didn't want to believe what I had just seen but I knew that it was most likely true. I typed in the page name that I was looking for and it was all in my face. My heart was so broken. I had done so much wrong in life and I swear karma came back in all kinds of ways. I stared at the rest in peace post just waiting for it to disappear like it had just been a figment of my imagination.

I jumped up and ran to my hall closet. I couldn't stay here. I grabbed my luggage from the hall closet and drug it back into my room, I started pulling clothes and shoes from my closet and tossing them into my bag. I pulled all my drawers open and began throwing everything that I could into my bags. Tears were falling from my eyes and I had no time to wipe them away.

My phone started ringing as I was tossing my clothes into my luggage. I just stared at the screen because I didn't want to answer. I didn't want to talk to anybody. There wasn't shit that anybody could say that would make me feel better. I just needed to get my shit and get the hell up out of the Bay. My phone was ringing off the hook and I figured that it would be best to just answer now. I wasn't going to tell anybody that I was leaving or where I was going but I was getting the hell up out of here no matter what.

"Hello," I said as I answered Rhea's call.

She had called about six times already just to tell me something that I already knew. "How are you, Lo? I just heard the news and I wanted to make sure that you were good."

I shook my head, unable to even respond to what she had just asked me. I wiped the tears from my eyes and dropped down to the floor next to my bed. "This is just too much, Rhea. Like what the fuck? None of this was supposed to happen. I know that we aren't together but this shit hurts my heart. Like death is just so real and I never felt a pain like this before," I said as I lay my head back against my bed. My heart ached so bad and I honestly couldn't have moved if I wanted to. My head was spinning and my heart was racing. I just knew if I made the smallest motion that I would throw up all over the place.

"Even though you and Diontay weren't together, that doesn't mean shit. Love has no titles or boundaries. Y'all spent time together and what's understood doesn't need to be explained so fuck who got something to say, Loren," Rhea said.

I shook my head as the tears continued to flow. "I'm pregnant," I said. It wasn't something that I had said out loud to anybody else so it came out as a whisper.

"Wait, you are what now?" Rhea asked, slightly raising her voice.

This time I said it a little louder. "I said I'm pregnant, and it's Diontay's baby. What will my baby and I do if he is gone? Why would they take him away from us? Who would do this Rhea? Who?" I yelled into the phone.

We sat there in silence as I cried my heart out. Rhea didn't say anything to me and I didn't say anything to her. I was grateful to have her on the phone with me but I had no words. I just thought back to that night. I just wanted to kiss him so damn bad. I could smell his body all around me and I just wished I could kiss his full lips one more time.

"Rhea, I don't even know what happened to him. Who did this?" I asked, sobbing into the phone.

"I don't know, Jaeda. They said it happened about five blocks from the club. Some people are saying that it was some Oakland niggas that were retaliating on some old beef that had popped off a couple of years ago. They said that Oakland had been fonkin' with them Richmond niggas for a cool little minute and they finally caught up with Tay and Quise."

I shook my head as I prayed that the people that took my baby's father away would rot in hell for what they had done. "So he never even left the club? That's fucked up, Rhea!" I said. This was all just too much for me. I was sick and I was pissed that I would never see him again and he died not even knowing that he had a child on the way. My ass was so busy playing games that I never told him.

"They say them niggas is called Gas Mobb, Team or something like that. You know I don't know these street gangs like that. I remember the old school gangs like S.T.I, M.N.B, Tree Girls, Hyfee Boys and Lacy Girls and shit like that. Hold on, Lo. This my mama on the other line. Don't hang up."

Chapter 13: Dolo

I was on the phone with Henah in hopes that she would give me a break and stop treating me like a redheaded stepchild. She wasn't breaking though and out of all the bitches that I fucked around with, I had grown to low-key like her pretty ass. We had seen each other a couple of times since Cabo and she was just hella cool to be around but it was apparent that I had blown my chances with her and she wasn't giving in. It was past three in the morning and I was on the phone begging a bitch that wasn't in the same city as me for the time of day. After I hung up, I checked myself because this shit wasn't even me. I didn't chase these bitches at all and I was tired of stepping outside of my character for this broad, so I deleted her number and placed my phone back in my pocket.

Jaeda had walked inside Denny's to go grab our food almost 30 minutes ago and she still hadn't returned. I turned around and shook Tamia. "Aye, T, I'm about to go check on Jae real quick." She mumbled something and dozed back off. I shook my head and laughed because it was funny to me how most females were always falling asleep in the car after the club.

I stepped out of the truck and walked around the building to the front of the restaurant. It was so packed that we decided to just get our food to go. We couldn't even park in the regular parking lot. Soon as I got close to the front of the building, I noticed a small crowd had gathered and they were huddled over somebody on the ground. I was about to just mind my business and walk past but you already know niggas always got to be nosey. I looked over one of the bystanders shoulders and my heart dropped to my damn stomach. I pushed through the crowd to get to Jaeda.

"That's my fucking sister! What the hell happened?" I yelled as I grabbed Jaeda's body out of the hands of the stranger that was holding her and applying pressure to her torso and chest where I could see blood coming from. I hadn't heard any gunshots so I wanted to know what the hell had happened.

I turned to the crowd and pulled the arm of the person who was holding Jaeda a minute ago. "Did you see what happened?" I asked the young girl that was kneeling down next to me now.

"Not really," she said. "I saw the end of it. She was fighting with another girl in the parking lot and then she went down. The girl ran off and I didn't realize that your sister had been stabbed until I walked up on her. I only knew something was wrong because from what I had seen, your sister was getting the best of the girl and for her to just drop like that was strange and then it took her way too long to get up. I'm so sorry," she said, looking at me with sad eyes.

I nodded my head as I looked up and saw the paramedics approaching and Tamia running over with a look of terror on her face. "Sir, I'm going to need you to step back so we can assess her injuries and get her stabilized and to the hospital." I moved back and filled Tamia in on what was happened as we watched the paramedics work on Jaeda. "Excuse me, sir. Are you related to the victim?"

I nodded my head. "Yes, that's my sister and this is our cousin," I said to the paramedic that was now standing directly in front of me and Tamia.

"Alright, well we are rushing her to Highland Hospital. You are welcome to ride to the hospital with her or you can meet us there, but we need to move quickly," the tall blonde medic said.

"We will meet you there," I said and she shook her head and rushed back to the ambulance that they were loading Jaeda into. Tamia and I ran back to my truck and hopped in. I pulled out of the parking lot and hit the gas headed to the hospital. My mind was racing. We had just killed that nigga Tay less than three hours ago and from what I knew, there wasn't really anybody left in his crew that would come back on some retaliation shit and not obviously that fast. So I needed to know who this bitch was that had stabbed my fucking sister. I was heated and I needed some fucking answers.

We pulled up to the hospital and found a parking space. Because it was early morning, it was easy to find something close. My heart was beating so hard and I was sick to my stomach. I was kicking myself in the ass because while I was on the phone talking to a bitch, my sister was getting done dirty by a punk rock ass bitch that should have been gotten her ass beat for that shit she pulled a few months back.

"I group texted the whole squad and told them to meet us up here. I ain't tell them nothing because I didn't need anybody freaking out."

I just nodded my head. I was so deep into my own thoughts that I had forgotten that she was even with me. Shit, I was walking so fast that I was surprised that she was even keeping up with her short ass legs. She looked worried as hell. I remember how Jae had told me that for the first year that they lived with their uncle, that her and her sister couldn't stand the twins. Looking at how close they were now, you would never know that there ever used to be any hostility between them.

As soon as we entered into the emergency room, Tamia ran to the triage station to find out where Jaeda had been taken and what was going on with her. "Excuse me, hey, I was waiting for you guys to arrive. Your sister is being rushed into surgery and soon as she goes into recovery, a doctor will be out to talk to you. I really hope that she pulls through and recovers quickly. She's definitely a fighter."

I nodded my head and extended my hand to the blonde medic that I had talked to back in the parking lot. I appreciated the fact that she had waited for us to arrive and filled us in because she could have easily left. "Thank you very much," I said as Tamia and I took a seat in the waiting area waiting for the doctor and the rest of the squad. I placed my head in my hands trying to process everything. It had been a long ass fucking day.

I looked up just in time to see Jamiya, Gio and China as they were coming over to where we were with worried expressions on their faces. I didn't want to have to keep telling the story over and over so I let them know we would wait until everyone had arrived before I ran down what had happened. A few minutes later, Rico, Greg, B, Daisy and Q all came piling in. Because there were so many of us, the hospital security came over and moved us into a private waiting room. I looked around and everybody had somber looks on their faces. After explaining what had taken place in the Denny's parking lot, we were all trying to process the severity of the situation, especially because the doctors had yet to come out and tell us anything.

I stood up and placed the floor. "Gio, Q, can I holla at y'all right quick?" I said as I started walking out of the waiting room and into the hallway. Q and Gio followed me and stood staring at me waiting for what I had to say. "Jae and I made a move on Richmond Tay earlier tonight," I said as I watched the both of their facial expressions change. "It happened so fast, my nigga. We were in the club turning up and then by the time we were leaving, Jae said she spotted them niggas in the club. As we were walking to the car, Tay and his nigga were like 100 yards in front of us and Jae called the play. Shit, we got in motion and executed in under five minutes," I said as Gio nodded his head.

He actually looked relieved. I knew that it was a sensitive subject for him and I could understand him being relieved. This nigga Tay had killed his brothers and had walked around for a couple of years like he was God himself. The nigga had gotten real comfortable in his motions and I guess he thought shit was sweet. I hadn't really had to bust my gun in a minute but that didn't mean shit because I was trained and ready to go at all times. I didn't give a damn how legit I went. I always kept it on me. It was better to have it and not need it than to need it and not have it. Fuck that.

Q leaned against the wall as he stared at the wall in front of him. "So were there any witnesses? Are y'all for sure that there wasn't anybody that could pinpoint you at the scene? Wasn't nobody following you, none of that?" Q asked in a low voice.

I shook my head. "Nah, cuzzo. I'm positive. We were on crunch time but we were most definitely on point. Tamia was the lookout but Jae and I had our eyes open the entire time."

Both Q and Gio nodded their heads, but I knew they were all wondering how in the hell Jae got fucked up. "Was there anything else that was off during the night?" Gio asked.

I thought about it and nodded my head. "You know what? When we were in the club, I saw Jae and Tamia exchanging words with some bitches when they were on the dance floor, but I didn't recognize them at all. It looked like it was going to escalate for a minute but then they all just walked away."

We all just sat there in silence for a moment. It was possible that Jae had run into the bitches again but for now we were at a standstill. The three of us walked back into the waiting room and sat down waiting for some kind of word.

Chapter 14: Big Money Q

As we all sat in the waiting room in the hospital, I was stuck. I didn't know what kind of shape Jae was in and I just prayed that she was going to pull through because I had so much planned for our future and she didn't even know it yet. I lay my head back against the wall that my chair was against and closed my eyes. I didn't know what had happened but I knew that Jaeda was a fighter. She had been through so much. She endured pain, grief, disappointments and everything in between. At the end of the day, I wasn't perfect but from the moment I laid eyes on Jae's little pretty ass, I just wanted to be perfect for her.

I looked up as the door to the waiting room swung open. The doctor had finally come in after over an hour and a half of waiting. We all gave the short Asian man our attention as he progressed towards us whole looking over his chart. "Hello, my name is Dr. Chu and this is the family of Jaeda Johnson, correct?" he asked and we all shook our heads and waited for him to continue. I was practically holding my breath waiting for the doctor to start talking. I could feel my anger rising as he continued looking over the chart. I wished he would just tell us what the fuck was going on already. "So Jaeda came into the hospital with multiple wounds from a knife or blade of some sort. Some of the wounds were only flesh wounds while a few of them were a bit more serious. After rushing Ms. Johnson into surgery, we were able to assess her appropriately and pinpoint the critical injuries. "

"So, Doc, can you tell us how bad the more serious wounds were and how many there were?" China asked.

"Ah, yes, the patient arrived with punctures to her brachial artery, a severed nerve in her upper forearm and a puncture to her left lung. We were able to stabilize her and repair all of the damage but she will definitely need to stay in the hospital for a week or two. There will be long lasting nerve damage to her arm that will heal over time but until it is fully healed, she will endure sharp pain, numbness and also dullness that will be very uncomfortable. Her lungs will heal over the next few weeks but she will experience times where she will be very short of breath. Any overexertion for a while will be tough for her, so I advise that as her family, you keep a close eye on her. No heavy lifting, long walking or even heavy exercise for the next six months or so." Dr. Chu removed his glasses and looked at us all. "Ms. Johnson has been through quite a bit of trauma so she was given a substantial dose of morphine for pain. She had a total of

76 stitches, some in her facial area, the neck area but mostly the neck and arm area. I would advise that you let her rest for now and then come back later today."

I let out a breath of relief. I was glad that Jae was okay. God knows I was up in this bitch sweating bullets over her ass. I didn't want to leave her ass, though. Sleep or not, I didn't want her to wake up and think that nobody was there for her. I pulled the doctor to the side and asked if I was able to stay with her. After getting the okay from the doctor, I spoke to the rest of the squad and let them know that I would be staying at the hospital until Jaeda woke up and I would also be staying in the Bay for the next couple of weeks while she was healing. Everybody knew how I felt about Jaeda. Despite the fact that I was with Laniece before, Jaeda was my heart and she probably didn't even know it. Her ass could ignore the chemistry we had if she wanted to but shit, I planned on bringing her up to speed. That girl was going to be mine no matter what I had to do.

I finished chopping it up with the squad and once everybody left, I headed in the direction of Jae's room. I promised to let everybody know once Jaeda woke up. Even though I knew that she was fine and would recover with no extreme damage, I still couldn't relax. I walked into the room and just stared at her face. She had bandages all over the place due to the multiple wounds but even through that, she was still beautiful to me. The scars would heal and she would be back to her old self over time but I definitely would be there every step of the way to make sure that she bounced back 100%. I pulled the pull out chair close to her bed and grabbed the extra linen from the small cabinet by the bathroom. I sat down and just stared at her. It was after 7 in the morning and I was tired as hell.

I felt my phone vibrate in my pocket. I pulled it out and looked at the text. I shook my head, tired of the bullshit. Laniece had been blowing me up and I didn't understand why she didn't get the point. This hoe ass bitch had cheated on me with multiple niggas and to make it worse, it was lame ass niggas from my city. The bitch traveled all over so if she was fucking three niggas from Oakland, there's no telling what niggas she was or had fucked in other cities. I didn't want an easy bitch that was for everybody. Shit, according to what I knew from all the messages, the bitch had a body count and I would never be attached to a dirt bag bitch like that. I was a real nigga through and through. I'd fucked with hella bitches before when I was a youngster in the streets. I fucked with hella bitches when I'd first started getting money on the level I was now and shit, I still had a few hoes online that I could call and they would be ready to do whatever whenever but no matter what I did, I didn't want a bitch that could match my body count and I couldn't trust Laniece so I didn't understand why she even kept trying to work some shit out with me. I was puzzled, really. Like bitch, come on. You already fucked up and made yourself look like a hoe in my eyes, so she needed to cut her losses and go get with one of them lame ass niggas that wanted her ass because I was done there was no turning back for me. I knew what I wanted and I wasn't going to stop until I got it.

I pushed my weight back and reclined the chair so that I was now laying back. I pulled the thin covers over my body and closed my eyes with thoughts of Jaeda at the forefront. I knew it would take time but she was the one that I wanted to bear my children and take on my last name. We had been playing the friend card for too long and I was ready to take this shit further. I knew she would give in to a nigga eventually but it was definitely going to take some time. Jaeda had been hurt too much and way too deep. She had a lot of demons that she dealt with on the daily. She tried to act like she was good but whenever I was around her, I could always feel her mood shift when she started thinking about her past.

I wasn't a stupid nigga. I knew that to penetrate her heart in the way that she had penetrated mine, I was going to have to have a lot of patience and come all the way correct. After the shit she went through with Chris, Jaeda was not in the business of giving up her heart or trusting easily. I knew that the death of her son killed her every day but I just wanted to be there to make her better. I drifted off to sleep saying a prayer for Jaeda and myself and the rest of my loved ones. I felt a storm brewing but I prayed that God wouldn't send anything my way that I couldn't handle.

I opened my eyes and stared into Jaeda's brown eyes. I could feel her eyes burning holes into me as I slept. I straightened up and stretched. I hadn't had a sleep that uncomfortable since my days on the block.

"You an old sucka for love ass nigga. Shouldn't your single ass be out fucking some bitches or something instead of laid up with me like a fake ass romance movie?" Jaeda said.

I laughed hella hard. It was funny as hell how her ass could always talk shit no matter the occasion. Jaeda let out a low chuckle and began coughing. Her cough was low and short but now it looked like she was in a lot of pain and was having trouble breathing. I hit the call button on the side of the bed and placed the oxygen back up to her nose. The doctor had said that she would have difficulty breathing.

I shook my head as I sat back down. "All that shit talking and your ugly ass can't even breathe. You better be nice to me, considering I'm going to be taking care of you while you are recovering," I said just as the nurse walked in.

I sat back as the nurse started checking Jaeda's vitals. "Hi Jaeda, I'm Tracy, your nurse for the next twelve hours. We just did a shift change so you're stuck with me for the rest of the day," she said as she looked back and winked at me. I looked away and stared at Jaeda. The nurse was a cute mixed chick but she wasn't anything to write home about. Bitches were bold as fuck. Here I was, laying up in the room with Jaeda and she was winking at me, trying to flirt while she supposed to be doing her job. After assessing Jaeda's pain level, she administered more morphine and explained that for the next couple of days, she would remain pretty drugged up due to the intensity of pain that her body will be enduring throughout recovery. I sent out a group text to let everybody know that Jae was awake.

About an hour later, the whole squad was up there to visit. I hung around for a minute but took the opportunity to go handle a couple of things before I came back later on. My first stop was to my house. I pulled up and walked through the front door. I was tired as shit and I really just wanted to climb in my bed and sleep but I had some shit to take care of. I walked into my home office and sat down at my desk. I pulled a bag of some bubblegum Kush and a bag of purple out of my drawer and smelled both. I thought on it for a second and decided to roll me up some purp. I pulled out some honey berry 1882s and rolled up. It had been a long morning and I needed something to ease my mind.

I powered up my desktop and logged into my email. I sent an email out to all of my shop managers and my café manager letting them know that I would be away for a few weeks but I would be checking in twice a week with conference calls to check on things. I let them know that it was a family emergency and it was business as usual until I came back. I would still be able to work out of my shop that I had out here in the Bay but my other two shops and café would be under the supervision of my appointed managers until I felt like Jae was well enough for me to leave her side.

I checked the books on all of my businesses to make sure that everything was straight and then sent all necessary documents over to payroll. After about two hours, I had wrapped up all of my necessary business. I had a move to make in about an hour and I needed to get my mind right. I sent a text to Dolo and Rico to see where they were. I knew they should have left the hospital by now. I sat back and sparked up another blunt. I lay my head back against the leather chair and thought about where I wanted to be in five years and it was crazy because I pictured Jaeda there with me in the future.

Ding dong, ding dong. I let out a loud breath as the doorbell rang. Dolo had keys to my house so I was wondering who the hell this could be. I wasn't expecting anybody but Dolo and Gotti so I got up and walked to the front door, spraying some Febreeze through the hallway as I went. I opened the door and was standing face-to-face with Laniece's thot ass. I shook my head as I leaned against the door frame staring at her, waiting on her to explain why her retarded looking ass was standing on my porch like she belonged there.

She cleared her throat like she was fishing for words. "Man, bitch, what the fuck do you want? You must be retarded as fuck to be standing on my doorstep. You lucky I didn't knock your head off the last time I saw you but clearly, you just want to keep testing my patience," I said as I stood straight up and looked directly in her eyes. This bitch just looked desperate as hell and I was disgusted that I had even wasted my time dealing with this weak ass hoe.

"You don't have to talk to me like that, Quinton. Why can't we just have a conversation like adults?" she had the nerve to say to me.

I smirked a little as I thought about how to address her. "Laniece, all bullshit to the side, I ain't got an ounce of respect left for your ass. You played the role like you was this goody two-shoes ass bitch, looking down on everybody else, accusing me of cheating on you and hella shit and your dirty ass was fucking on multiple niggas and coming back to me with some dry ass pussy that you wasn't even throwing at me on the regular. And let's not even get on that bunk ass head you was serving. Bitch, so miss me because this shit is done and there ain't no getting back for us. Not now, not ever."

I walked away from the door and grabbed the plastic tub that I had put all of Laniece's things in and walked back to the door, throwing it at her feet. Her dramatic ass jumped back like it was a snake or something, I turned back around and slammed the door behind me. I couldn't believe the bitch tried to play me like a lame nigga then going to come trying to talk like I was supposed to be over it after a couple of weeks, like I was some hoe ass nigga. That bitch must not have known the first rule of thumb. You can't play a playa. Fuck she thought she was? Better yet, who the fuck she thought I was? I walked into my bedroom and hopped in the shower. I had some business to take care of and the quicker I could get it over with, the quicker I could get back up to the hospital with Jae.

I had just thrown my clothes on when I heard the alarm being disarmed. I hurriedly grabbed my shoes because I knew Dolo's impatient ass was about to start rushing me. I had on one of those ugly ass brown UPS uniforms. I grabbed the badge and stuck it in the front of my shirt. Soon as I pulled on the brown beanie, I was ready to go. I walked into the hall closet and reached behind all of the clean linen as I punched in the code to my safe. Once the safe popped, I grabbed my .40 cal with the Laserguard and stuck it in my waistband and went into the front room where both Rico and Dolo were waiting for me in all black clothing. I nodded my head and grabbed my keys and phone and we were out the door. Even though I had gone legit and was getting money with my businesses, sometimes it was just hard to ignore the call of the streets. And when the payout was worth it, then I mean shit, what can I say?

The three of us hopped into the all-black Suburban and we were on our way. I plugged my phone into the auxiliary and turned on Nipsey's *Mailbox Money* and lit a blunt as we all rode and cleared our mind for the job ahead of us. After driving for a little over an hour, we were pulling up to an abandoned house in Sacramento. I hopped out of the Suburban and walked up to the UPS truck that was parked on the side of the house. My cousin Jew had left it unlocked. I placed the keys to the Burban underneath the driver's seat and the three of us hopped in the UPS truck. I locked in the address that he had sent me into my GPS and took off towards our destination.

The address we were directed to was about twenty minutes away from where we had picked the truck up from. It was a small storefront that stood alone at the end of a quiet street. My cousin gave us the run down on how everything should go down. The mark was an OG cat that received packages once a month in bulk. He owned a motorcycle gear shop and received bulk packages that contained pounds of weed. My cousin vouched that there were about twenty boxes that he received per delivery and out of the twenty boxes, ten of them contained a pound of weed in between packages of t-shirts. Our job was to hit the mark and my cousin had already set up the buyer for the pounds that we were going to get, so before we left out of Sac Town, the paper would be in our hands.

Jew would meet us about a block away from the shop where we would switch vehicles and be back on the way.

I pulled up and backed the truck all the way to the roll up door that was on the side of the building, I hopped out of the truck with the clipboard in hand and rang the bell on the side wall. After a few seconds, the door lifted and I was standing face to face with a baldheaded older cat. He wasn't very bulky but he wasn't a small nigga, either.

"Hello, I have a delivery for a Mr. Samuel Casper," I said as I stepped inside the small storage room. I took a quick glance around.

"Yeah, that's me. Where's the other guy that usually comes and does the deliveries?" he asked.

I handed him the clipboard for him to sign and once he had handed me the clipboard back, I turned my back and began to unload the truck. I shot a text to Jew and let him know that we were in. Rico and Dolo had already finished stripping the boxes and loaded the P's into duffle bags that Jew had placed in the back of the truck. Rico stripped the boxes of the product and Dolo had resealed the boxes. This lick was light work compared to some shit that we did but we always had to stay on our toes. The OG walked out of the back storage room as I started stacking boxes over in the corner. From outside of the truck, you couldn't see Rico and Dolo crouched down inside.

I continued to unload the boxes like I really worked for this damn company or something. We didn't have any intentions on having to hurt the OG but for our safety and for the sake of the money that was on the line, we had brought our bangers just in case. If all went as planned, we would be leaving just as quietly as we had come. I was stacking the last couple of boxes when the OG came back from the front of the store and began opening up the boxes. I didn't expect for him to start opening the boxes until after we were already gone but if shit got sticky, we were going to rock with it however it went. "Alright, Mr. Casper. My job here is done, you have a great day," I said as I started walking back towards the front of the truck.

"Hold tight, young man. Why do these boxes look like they have been tampered with?" he said as he began walking towards me.

I turned around to face him and he began walking towards me aggressively but I stood my ground and remained levelheaded, as if I didn't know what he was talking about. I plastered a look of concern on my face. "I am not sure why you say that, sir, but I can assure you that there was no tampering of the parcels," I said as I waited for him to respond.

"Well, I don't give a damn what you are assuring me, but I am telling you what the fuck I know and I know that my boxes were opened before they got here," he said aggressively as he walked up on me.

Soon as I got ready to open my mouth, Dolo and Rico hopped out of the truck with their bangers drawn. "Nah, playboy. Back that shit on up. Get them hands up, my nigga," Rico said as he walked up on the OG and began patting him down.

I pulled my banger as well and trained it on the mark's head. "Put your nose against the wall, homie. Y'all run through this bitch," I said as I held my gun against the back of the nigga's head. We knew that the nigga was holding some dough and shit inside but we had really only come for the ten Ps but since he wanted to veer from the plan, we were about to take it all, life included. Fuck this nigga.

I looked at my watch and we had about ten minutes to get the fuck up out of this bitch before Jew would be calling me to see where we were. "I should have known something was up. Jewelz never misses a delivery day and I pay him heftily to make sure that he doesn't," said the OG.

I smirked. "Well, today he did and you still paying heftily, so how about you focus on making things right with God before you leave this Earth, my nigga." I hit the nigga in the back of the head with the butt of my gun. I backed up as he fell to the ground. A couple of seconds later, Rico and Dolo were running from the front of the store with a duffle bag each. I sent two to the nigga's head and we got the fuck up out of there. I hit the button on the wall on the way out and made sure that the roll up door closed behind me. The shop was already closed from the front so it would be a minute before anybody even found the nigga.

I pulled up to the spot that we were supposed to be meeting Jew and I hopped out of the UPS truck with my niggas behind me. Jew hopped out of the Suburban just as an older model minivan pulled up next to him. Two young Asian niggas hopped out and stood next to the van watching Jew and I. I pulled Jew to the side and let him know that shit kind of went left and we had to do what we had to do. Jew was my cousin and even though he had squared up and gotten a job, he knew what came with the game so he wasn't tripping. He turned towards the Asians and nodded his head. They then opened the back doors to the Suburban and placed the bags inside. Dolo had let me know that both duffle bags were filled with money. I tossed both to Jew and he tossed me one back and let me know that the guys had placed the dough for the Ps in my trunk underneath my spare. I nodded to him and we were out just like that.

We came off pretty cool from this lick. I was sure it could have gone smoother but we weren't about to go back and forth with the possibilities. What's done was done and now I was focused on making this drive smoothly back to the Town so I could get back up to the hospital with Jaeda. I had been gone about six hours and I knew that Tamia was ready to go so she could hit the block. Now that the job was done, we could relax a little so we started making small talk.

I missed these times sometimes, just being in the field with my niggas making moves. Gotti used to always run with us a few years ago. It used to be me, Dolo, Gotti and Gio and on some occasions, we would put Tone and Jah up on some moves. As much as I liked being legit, I loved the rush of hitting a lick because that shit was like oxygen to my lungs. I was a nigga straight out of the gutter and it would always be in a nigga to get his hands dirty every once in a while.

"Aye, man. I got some shit to tell you niggas," Dolo said as he popped open a bottle of white Remy while we were stuck in traffic passing through Berkeley. I hated passing through here because no matter what time of day you came you, would always hit some kind of traffic.

"What's up, nigga?" Rico asked.

I looked over at Dolo and waited for him to get to talking but he looked nervous, like he was about to tell us some deep shit. "Nigga, the fuck you got to tell us? Don't tell me your nasty ass done caught some shit you can't get rid of," I said as I gave him a wondering look.

"Well shit, I guess I won't tell you then," he said.

I hit the brakes, damn near hitting the car in front of me. "Nigga, the fuck you mean?" I said, damn near yelling.

"Yeah, nigga, what you talking?" Rico asked. I was tired of this nigga beating around the bush and he needed to just say whatever he had to say and do it quick.

Dolo shook his head and just stared at me for a second. "Man, cuzzo, I found out last night that I got a baby on the way," he said like he had just lost his best friend.

I burst out laughing because this nigga did all of that over a motherfucking baby. "Nigga, that's all? Shit, I thought you was about to say you caught that Eazy-E or some shit," I said, but he still was looking all down and shit.

"Man, I'm pissed the fuck off because the bitch is ugly as fuck, my nigga. I fucked up big time. Like nigga, I'm really that nigga and I ain't ever been caught with nothing less than a bad bitch but that night in Cabo when I dipped off, I got caught up and now that shit just came back and bit me in my ass." I shook my head at this nigga. He was hella cocky. I didn't think that it could have been that bad. "Gotti, remember the night we dipped off? Remember the cousin that was hella black but she was thick as fuck but her face was hurt as fuck?" Dolo turned towards the back to look at Rico.

"Hell yeah, I remember that bitch. She tried to bring her drunk ass in the room with me and suck my dick but I kicked her ass out with the quickness," Rico said, cracking up.

I started laughing so hard that I started choking and Rico started beating me on the back as I struggled to get it together. "So Gotti had enough sense to send the thot ass bitch on her way but even after you fucked two bitches, your nasty ass still hadn't gotten enough and you fucked her and now she's your baby mom's?" I said, shaking my head. Dolo was and had always been known to get around. That nigga would fuck a bitch quick but I thought he at least had some standards. After hearing this, I was starting to think my nigga was losing his touch.

"Man, y'all don't understand. that bitch came in and started sucking my dick with the force of an army, bruh, and I got so caught up in the moment watching her bob up and down on my shit that I just pushed that bitch's face down, ass up but I fucked up running up in her raw and now she refuses to get an abortion. Man, I got the worst luck." Dolo was tripping. I passed him the bottle back and exited the freeway heading back to my spot.

Chapter 15: Jaeda

I woke up from a long nap and just laid here staring at the ceiling. I just wanted to go home. I had gone out to celebrate a new chapter in life and now here I was laid up in a hospital bed with cuts and stab wounds. My chest was on fire, every breath I took felt like needles to my lungs. I didn't want to shed any tears but I didn't understand why life was proving to be so fucking hard for me. They say when you are going through shit that there are people out there that are dealing with worse. My thing was this, when I was dealing with pain, suffering and loss I was not worried about nobody else and their fucking issues. I was grateful to be alive after all of the things that I had been through but I was so tired of all the drama, the ills of the street life, the loss and most importantly, pain.

I was lying in the dark of my hospital room. Everybody had left earlier and I was glad to be by myself. I thought back to the day that I'd had, from going to the club and catching yet another body to running into Lo at Denny's and fighting her ass. I couldn't believe that bitch had stabbed me. I didn't know if she was really trying to take my life or what but I knew that this wasn't over. I would hate to have to kill Lo but I was definitely going to put my foot all the way up in her ass the next time I caught up to that hoe. For now though, I would be sitting up in this bitch trying to get better. My body had better do its job and recover quickly because I had things to do and I wasn't going to be able to do it from this hospital bed.

I heard my room's door open but I didn't look to see who it was. I figured it was a nurse coming to check on me. The disruptions were never-ending in this place. I closed my eyes and inhaled Q's cologne as he approached my bed and sat down in the chair next to it. "Why does your ugly ass keep coming up here like you're my nigga or something?" I asked as he let out a long yawn.

"Girl, shut your ass up. Shit, if your lonely ass had a nigga then I could be at home or something, instead of up here babying your ungrateful ass," Q said as he leaned over and kissed me on the cheek.

I raised my eyebrows and looked at Q as he sat back down. The light from the hallway was shining into my room so it wasn't completely dark inside. The light was shining on his face and I was stuck just staring at him. Being in Q's presence always did something to me. It was like he was always able to pull the strings of my heart a little whenever he was around.

It had been a few years since I had first met Quinton Stewart and from the moment that I laid eyes on him, I knew he was that nigga. At the time, I was in a relationship with Chris and he didn't have anybody. He was always great with my son and was just somebody that I knew from the beginning would always be someone that I could count on. With meeting Q, I had also gotten really close to Dolo and with the both off them in my life, I felt blessed. It was crazy because I constantly compared niggas to Tone. I had never gotten over my first love and I didn't believe that I ever would but I could say that I had honestly never been able to compare Tone and Quinton. They both were the realest niggas I had ever came across. Their auras exuded leadership and there was no doubt about it that if Tone's life had not been cut short, that he would be a boss and king of this city. Tone would always hold the key to my heart but I had no problems exploring the thought of letting Q get the spare key.

"How are you feeling, Jae Money?" Q asked.

I thought for a minute because honestly, I felt like shit but I didn't want his continuous pity. "Honestly, Q, I just want to be alone. I feel like shit but I don't want to be around anybody. Thanks for coming up here and being with me and shit, but you can go and live your life. I told everyone earlier that I didn't want them coming up here. I will see everybody once I come home," I said, holding back tears. My body was in so much pain and I didn't have the energy to keep trying to hold back these breakdowns. My emotions were everywhere and I just needed this time to deal with everything. So much had happened over the years and I just had to reevaluate everything around me. I had taken the steps to make the necessary changes in life but it seemed as if bullshit just followed me everywhere that I went. I wanted a new start because karma was a bitch and I was tired of looking over my shoulder, scared that it was coming around to fuck with me.

Q just stared at me for a minute before he said anything. I couldn't read the look on his face. I didn't know if he was mad or upset but I just wanted him to respect my feelings and go home. Q shook his head and stood up to leave. He leaned down and kissed my forehead as he usually did and then winked at me as he walked towards the door. "I know you need time to get your mind right, Jae Money, but despite what you think you are going through alone, I'm always here. Hopefully one day you will see that you got me and quit running from a nigga."

I stared at him for a second and let out a deep breath and as much as I wanted to hold in my tears until he walked out, they had their own agenda because they came pouring out on their own free will. It was if every emotion that I had bottled up came pouring out of my eyes. I didn't even feel any physical pain at the moment, just the pain that was deep in my heart, the emptiness and despair that was deep in my gut.

Quinton came rushing to my side and threw his body around me. I had completely broken down. I didn't think I had ever had this big of a breakdown throughout everything that I had been through over the last few years. When Sage, my sister, Tone and Jah were killed, I never really had the moment to let it all out. When Baby Tone was killed, I went through a really dark time but it was nothing like this. My best friend, uncle, aunt and cousin were all doing time and that fucked with me every day and I still relived the night that my father drove us into the lake. So this moment was a long time coming. It was a moment where every raw emotion came pouring out without permission. I cried so hard that I was heaving and there was snot and tears everywhere. I wanted Q out of there because I knew that I was bottling all this up and I had hit that final breaking point. I hadn't wanted anybody to witness this but at the moment, I was actually very grateful that he was here.

After about fifteen minutes of uncontrollable crying, the tears had finally ceased, but my chest was literally on fucking fire. I couldn't breathe and my mouth was dry as hell. I reached for the water pitcher with my good arm and it was still hella painful. Q grabbed the pitcher from me and poured me a cup of water as I placed the oxygen back in my nose and lay back on the bed. I was exhausted mentally and physically.

"You better now, Jae? I mean, do you feel like you let everything out finally? After all of this time, do you feel like you finally are able to move past everything that you have been through?" Q said as he sat on the side of my bed and rubbed my hand.

I thought about it for a moment and shook my head. There weren't really many words to say but I honestly did feel as though a huge weight had been lifted from my shoulders. I was finally ready to let go and move the hell on with my life. I didn't want to just ignore the pain. I was ready to move past it all. I nodded my head, looking into Q's eyes. "Yeah, Quinton, I'm ready. I honestly have been holding in everything since the day we laid Sage to rest. Since that very day, everything has been a straight fucking whirlwind and I know that I have been all over the place these last few years but I thank you for every day that you have been there for me and stood behind me pushing me to be a better me." I lay my head back and stared at the ceiling. "I'm finally ready to move on with life and be happy, and I never felt like I was allowed to be happy because I felt as though I was leaving my family behind. I felt guilty for my son's death and I felt like I owed Tone my heart and dedication but now, after all this bullshit, I finally realize that I can't bring anybody back and that I can't keep living in darkness. It's my duty to live my life to the fullest and honestly, Quinton, I really just want somebody that is going to be here with me and for me. Someone that I can really just live with. I love being around you and Dolo and just the whole squad, but I am also ready to have the family and life that I always dreamed of," I said.

Q reached over and rubbed the side of my face as a lone tear fell down my cheek. "I feel you, Jae, but can I ask you something?" I looked at Q and nodded my head, eager to find out what he wanted to ask me. "You know I been feeling your lil ass for a minute, man. Literally since the very first day that I laid my eyes on you. So I really just want to know if you ready to fuck with a nigga or not? Shit, you know me and I know that pussy, so what's up?" he asked with a huge grin on his face.

I laughed as much as I could in my condition. I swear this nigga was always playing but it was cute. "Nigga, please. Just because you had this good shit doesn't mean you know it. You got a whole lot to learn, my nigga," I said, closing my eyes and thinking about what Q had just asked me. Did I really want to try and be with him? I didn't really know if I could be that woman that he was looking for but honestly I was tired of denying my feelings for this man. I might have been unsure but I wasn't stupid. Q was a good ass man and I didn't want to see another bitch get him and I be kicked back wondering what could have been.

Before I could answer, my nurse came in to check my vitals and administer my pain meds. "Hi, Jaeda, how are you feeling?" Tracy asked me as she walked in and wrote down my vitals on her chart. She pulled her small cart close to the bed and explained that she was about to change my bandages.

I stared at Q for a while as Tracy moved around me, changing each bandage on my body. I just soaked up all of his energy because honestly, I needed his positivity. If he believed in me, then I needed to believe in myself just as much.

"My shift is over so Christa will be the nurse taking over in an hour or so. On a scale of 1-10, what is your pain level?" she asked as she changed out my I.V. and then glanced at Q. She had tried her best to not look his way since the first time she came in this morning but I knew it was hard for her. Shit, Quinton was fine as fuck and any woman in her right mind would look at his ass. "Like a strong 7 and my chest feels extremely heavy but I don't know if the pain in my arm or my chest is worse. It's kind of all blending together now," I said as I lifted slightly while Q fixed my pillows behind my head.

"Okay, well, I am going to give you a little extra dose of pain medicine. It will definitely have you out for the rest of the night. I'm also going to administer these antibiotics into your IV. The doctor just wants to decrease the chance of infection. You will feel a little sting as it hits your veins but only for a small second." I nodded my head and let her handle her business.

Once Tracy had finished she said her goodbyes and left the room, I looked at Q but my eyes were heavy as fuck. I smiled a weak smile and his ass started laughing. "Blood, your ass is high, I ain't fucking with you," he said.

I shook my head weakly. "You ain't got to fuck with me but I'm fuckin' with you, Mr. Stewart. We can take shit slow but I'm definitely fuckin' with yo' ass," I said as my eyes dropped and I used all my strength to open them back up. "You don't have to stay, boo. Go home and come back in the morning," I said to him. He leaned down and kissed my forehead, my nose and then my lips. I finally closed my eyes for good. I could hear him talking to me but I was too high and tired to piece together what he said. Hopefully, he didn't say anything too important because I was out for the count.

Chapter 16: Big Money Q

I woke up to my phone ringing. I tried to ignore it but I swear it was just ringing nonstop. I looked up at the clock on my nightstand and groaned. It was almost three in the morning. Whoever was calling better have had some money on the line. I'd had a long night and went to sleep not expecting to wake up until daylight.

I answered my phone and tried to adjust my eyes to the darkness as I listened to the caller on the other line of my phone. Soon as the caller was finished talking, I hopped out of bed and threw on some sweatpants and Jordans. I walked to my closet and grabbed a black pullover hoodie and then reached into the top of my closet and grabbed my bitch. I had a clean ass AK-47 and she was like my right hand in the streets. I grabbed my phone and keys and called my cousin Dolo as I snuck out the back door and walked around to the front of the house and down the block where my car was parked.

"Aye, bitch, wake yo' ass up. I'm about to come snatch yo' ass so be ready, nigga." I hung up the phone

and hopped in my all-black 50 or Mustang 5.0 as they were called and pulled off headed to Dolo's house. I had been hustling outside all day and I was tired than a bitch but my nigga Rico called and said he had a play up so when money called me and my niggas answered, no questions asked.

I was 19 and my crew was wild as fuck. We stayed on one and the definition of hyphy. Niggas knew who we were and most niggas steered clear of us but there was always that one nigga or one crew that thought that they were harder and decided to try us but at the end of the day, my niggas were really about that life. I pulled up to Dolo's house and blew my horn. D's mom, my auntie Pat, was never home this time of night unless she was crashing from a long week of binging but I knew her ass was gone. Shit, even if she wasn't, she wouldn't give a fuck about Dolo leaving out.

I waited for a couple of minutes until I finally saw Dolo running out of the parking lot of his apartments towards my whip. I reached over and unlocked his door and took off once he was in the car. I called Rico and let him know that I was pulling up any second. This lick was about to be like taking candy from a baby. Rico was the play master that's how he got the nickname Gotti, he was the one that usually got the drop did the homework and then put us up on the play. He was a couple of years younger than me and Dolo but that nigga was putting in work on the streets. Niggas knew blood and knew he didn't play around. If it made money, it made sense to that nigga.

Rico and I had been sitting on these niggas from the Hunnids for some weeks and it was finally time to make that move. These niggas were young, lazy niggas that tried to high power flex around the Town like they were really them niggas. No doubt about it, those niggas were doing numbers but they were some bootsy ass niggas that wouldn't bust the guns if their lives depended on it. They just liked to be flashy and fuck with hella bitches. They would bring hella bitches to the block and instead of watching the block, they would be too busy entertaining hoes. The nigga that was supposed to come through and collect the dough every couple of hours would always make the niggas hold onto the money and then would grab it from them in the morning instead of every three hours like they were supposed to. Rico had a cousin that fucked with one of the niggas and she put us up on game. If the money wasn't picked up that night then we knew those niggas were sitting on damn near ten stacks easy. It was the weekend and the third of the month, so we were about to come the fuck up.

I pulled up a block over and killed my engine. Rico hopped out of his whip and threw a ski mask to both me and Dolo. "Sup, my niggas? It's only two niggas over there and about three hoes. They drunk and high as fuck so you already know this is gonna be a piece of cake. Y'all take up the front and I'm going to come up behind them just in case one of them niggas try to grow wings. I ain't worried about the bitches because Trina out there and I already hit her up and let her know what time it was," Rico said as we all pulled on our masks. The streets were fairly quiet but you could hear traffic in the distance from the partygoers and niggas in the sideshow tearing the streets up.

Dolo and I took off running to the next block as Rico took off in the opposite direction. "Hands up, pussy! Where that paper at, nigga?" I yelled as I pulled my choppa and aimed it at the heavyset pretty boy. Soon as our guns came out, the bitches ran off and hopped in their car. Rico had already handled that shit so we didn't even have to worry about them hoes running their mouths.

"Man, ain't no money. My nigga came and picked it up already. We just out here chillin'," the tall skinny nigga said, looking like he was about to shit his pants.

I chuckled because these niggas really thought that they were about to play us. "Nigga, who do you think you talking to? You think me and my nigga just coming over here all blind, hoping for a come up? Nah, nigga. Either you go grab that paper or I will grab it myself and if I got to get it, then you won't make it to see another dollar, bitch," Dolo said.

The skinny nigga looked around and I knew he was looking for a way out. I moved closer to the niggas, gun still drawn and his ass broke. I looked up and Rico dropped that nigga with two shots. I looked at his patna and he had pee falling down his legs. I laughed. "Your bitch ass. Nigga, where that money at?" I asked and he pointed. Dolo went in the direction that he'd pointed in and opened up the car door to find a duffle bag full of money in the backseat. Dolo was about to close the door when he reached in and pulled another bag from the other side of the car.

Dolo ran back over to where I was and gave fat boy three to the chest and then threw me one of the duffle bags. The three of us took off running and made it back to our cars. I started up my car and followed Rico back to Dolo's spot. That was an easy lick compared to some of the plays we ran but that money was right. We had come up on fifteen stacks that night and a little weed. After that, I didn't even go back to sleep. I ate breakfast at Dolo's house and we hit the block like just another day.

I sat in my home office smoking and thinking about the old days. Dolo and Rico were my day one niggas. Dolo was my blood cousin and we had been rocking since Pampers but Rico had been our nigga since 9th grade at Emery and he was in the 7th. When we did our dirt, he was right there. We had all come a long way and I was proud of the men we had become, business owners and not in the streets still living reckless like we used to. Yeah, we still got our hands dirty from time to time but shit, it was all in the name of chasing after that almighty dollar. Niggas still had to eat and sometimes when you come from the gutter, you resort back to the shit that you came up doing.

I was living most niggas' dreams. I came and went when I felt like it and I owned two homes, businesses and all my whips were paid for. I could get up and travel to wherever the fuck I wanted when I wanted and I had plenty money to blow, from hustling to being legit, I had paved my way since I was a youngster and it had definitely paid off. Now I was to that point in my life where I was ready to settle down. I'd had a couple of relationships in the past but I never felt like they were going anywhere. I had my eyes fixated on my future though and I wasn't going to let it go.

Today was the day that Jaeda was due to come home from the hospital and I couldn't even lie, I was anxious as hell. She'd already told me that she was fuckin' with a nigga but I planned on showing her that she was really going to be my wife. Whether she knew it or not, she was the woman I was about to start my family with. I planned on rocking with her for the long haul. It was crazy because I was actually a little nervous. I had gone back to Vegas on a turnaround flight just to check on things at my shops and had returned earlier this morning so that I could be back before Jaeda was discharged. Greg was picking her up from the hospital but we were all going to be meeting at her house later on for a family dinner. This was different though because Jaeda was always around but we always had to keep our distance because of her relationship or mine but now all that shit was dead and I could be all up on her ass if I wanted to.

I shut down my computer and prepared myself to get up and get dressed. I had about two hours before it was time to head over to Jaeda's. The dinner started at 7 but I wanted to get there early so I could see Jaeda and get some alone time before everybody else arrived. Once I got dressed, I grabbed the gift bag from the mantelpiece and headed out of the door. I had this crazy anxious feeling about seeing Jaeda because it was like now I could finally just do what I wanted to do to her. I could kiss her, grab her ass, and whatever else when I wanted to and in front of whoever and not even have to worry about what anybody thought or said. The only thing that mattered to me now was making Jae happy and helping her to become the best woman that she could be. I already knew that she was the one for me, the beginning and the ending of me, but I was just waiting for her big headed ass to get that through her head.

I pulled up to Jae's house and saw Gio and China's Range pulled in the driveway. I parked on the curb and hopped out, grabbing the gift bag and pulling my Niners snapback down on my head. It was weeks away from Christmas and it was cold as hell outside today and raining on top of that, I hurried up the driveway to the front door trying my best to not get too soaked in the storm because it was really coming down.

I rang the doorbell and waited for somebody to come and let me in. I hadn't been to the hospital to see Jaeda in a few days and I couldn't wait to look into her beautiful face. It was crazy that I felt this way because just a couple of months ago, I was always away from Jaeda and even though I always missed her presence and thought about her constantly, it didn't feel anything like now. Now it was like I was having withdrawals from not being in her space. The time that we spent apart made my body tingle in anticipation of being near her again.

I looked up from my phone as Gio pulled the door open with Gioni in his arms and Charlie at his feet. I stepped in and grabbed the baby from his arms. "What's good, bruh?" I dapped Gio as we walked through the walkway towards the living room.

"Shit, my nigga, taking care of these kids. Jae and China are in the room. China was helping Jae get dressed," Gio said as we sat down in the living room. I looked down in my arms at Gioni and started talking to him. He was hella chunky and cute. That shit made a nigga think about having a few of my own.

As I sat there and played with the baby, I imagined what my own children would look like. I wanted three kids at the least, all with Jaeda's complexion and smile. Everything else was up in the wind but I could see three little mini versions of us running around. I thought about Baby Tone and felt sad that his life was cut short and he wouldn't be here to be loved by his future brothers and sisters. I had grown to love Baby Tone. I'd spent a lot of time with him during his short life due to being around Gio's spot a lot. Me and that little nigga had bonded from the very first day that I had ever spent around him and his mother. I hated that Chris' bitch ass had killed him. I couldn't even imagine the pain she felt daily because I knew just how bad I felt about it.

After a couple of minutes, Gioni was sleep in my arms. China walked in the room and came and grabbed him out of my arms. "I'm going to lay him down but you can go and see Jae. She's dressed but not ready to walk all the way in here yet. That shower took a lot of her energy," China said as she walked off towards the guest bedroom off to the side of the living room.

I nodded my head and got up to go see my girl. "Give me a minute, bruh. I'll be back down in a minute." I said with a smirk on my face.

"Aye, my nigga, your creep ass better not go in there trying to get nasty with my sister. Her breathing ain't even cool enough for all that. Don't make me beat your ass, Q," Gio said and we both laughed but I could tell that retarded ass nigga was serious as fuck.

I walked up the stairs and went into Jae's room as she was laying across the top of the bed on her laptop as she had Future's "Real Sisters" playing low. I looked at her and she actually looked peaceful. She had an oxygen tube in her nose and was dressed down in some multicolored yoga pants with a hot pink sports bra.

She looked up at me and smiled as I entered the room. Her soft perfume tickled my nose as I went and stood over her. I smiled and bent down to kiss her lips. Feeling her lips on mine was better than sex right now. Alright, maybe not better than sex but that shit was fire though. I pulled away and just stared at her for a second before I sat down next to her on the bed. "What's up, Jae Money? Why you got this tight ass shit on?" I asked, looking into her eyes that were staring right back into mine.

"Don't come in here trying to be all up in my space with them questions and shit like you my nigga or something," she said with her face frowned up.

"Fuck you mean, like?" I said as I moved closer to her on the bed to where our lips were damn near touching again. "I am your nigga, so go on with all that bullshit you talking, Jae. I'm your man and this is all me," I said as I grabbed her ass and kissed her, running my tongue across her lips. Jaeda shook her head and smiled as I leaned in to kiss her again but this time she backed up and had me looking dumb as fuck, leaned in trying to kiss her ass. I laughed at how she had just played me. "Oh, I see your little ass playing games already. I'm going to let you play for now but you better be cool because payback is a bitch and when I start playing, you might try and tap out," I said as I lay back on her bed with my hands behind my head.

Jaeda lay back with me as she snuggled up close to me, and closed her eyes. "Shut up, crybaby. I just was playing with your ugly ass. You waited until I got high off all of them pain meds and then forced me to be your broad. Now I can't break up with you because then I might hurt your feelings," Jaeda said, laughing lightly.

I laughed with her crazy ass. "I swear you got jokes for days. Just watch, nigga. I got you, Jae." I said, rubbing her stomach. I looked over at her and my eyes fell on all of the scars on her body.

Jaeda's upper body had endured a lot of pain over the past couple of weeks but most of her stitches had dissolved and she was healing pretty well but there was still evidence of what she had been through. I thought about the morning of Jae's attack and I remember how scared I was walking in that hospital and not knowing what had happened to her. I just remembered asking God to spare her life because I hadn't even had the chance to tell her how much I needed her in my life; shit, how much she needed me in her life. On some real shit, I was really that nigga and these lame ass niggas didn't compare and couldn't even keep up with a bitch like Jae. But me, nah, she was made for a nigga like me and God knew that. So I know that's why she was still here, just so that she could complete me.

I closed my eyes thinking about how to approach the conversation that I knew we needed to have. Well, I should say one of the more important ones. We needed to talk about a bunch of shit but for now, I needed to know where her head was at. I had my ear to the streets and I was hearing a lot of shit. Jae had only told China that Lo was the one to stab her that morning at Denny's. China had confided in me because Jae had told her not to tell anybody until she was out of the hospital but she had come to me about a week ago and put me up on game. I was ready to put that bitch in a body bag but I needed to know what Jae wanted to do.

"Jae, I already know you know that shit isn't about to go ignored, right? You already know that once everybody knows that Lo was behind this shit, there ain't shit you can say to stop motherfuckas from getting on her head, you feel me?" I said as I lay there waiting for her response.

She didn't look at me so I knew she wasn't surprised that I knew. I felt her take a deep breath before she began talking. "I'm already knowing, Quinton. hella days in that hospital I put together a million and one scenarios on how I was about to knock that bitch down but then some days I woke up like fuck it, move on and live my life," she said, shaking her head. I knew she wasn't finished speaking so I didn't respond. "I heard that bitch is pregnant by Tay. I think she has an idea that Gas Squad made that play on his ass. My niggas said she ain't even know it was the same Tay that killed my sister but whatever the case, she's salty over the fact that her baby is not going to have a daddy. I don't have the energy or mind frame to make that move, Q, but I gave Jamiya and her crew the green light because I know one day I'm going to wake up and feel like a dummy for letting her ass live. I would rather take her out before one day she wake up mad at the world and come at me on some salty shit. I know that it will bother me for a while but I will be okay with it eventually," she said and I nodded because I knew how she felt but we all knew that Lo just couldn't exist any longer. She had violated one too many times and her connection with Tay was the straw that broke the camel's back.

I lay there for one moment thinking before I said anything. Lo and Jae had history so I knew that it wouldn't be easy for her to just make a move on her like she was some random bitch. The only thing was that Jaeda was unpredictable with her feelings. Things that you would think would bother her didn't. It was like she just buried certain things and said fuck it. I think that if Lo wasn't tied to Tay, then Jae would have probably wanted everybody to let the shit go but with her being pregnant with the nigga, it sparked up a whole other feeling about her.

I turned on my side and faced Jaeda. Her eyes were closed and breathing unsteady so I know she was deep in thought. "What about the baby?" I asked. If we killed Lo, then her baby would be left in this world as an orphan. Either way, there would be guilt for how we carried the situation but the call was on Jaeda so I would stand beside her decision no matter what she decided.

"Honestly, I rolled around on a few different ideas and in order to spare the baby, we would have to wait another four months or so. Honestly, I don't want to sit on that bitch for that long. It will either give her time to sky up and disappear or time to make a move on me. Lo a square ass bitch but I ain't putting shit past an emotional ass bitch."

I nodded my head; she was right so I guess it was set. I was low-key glad that Jamiya was going to handle that shit. She hated Lo and I knew she wouldn't feel any type of way about the situation afterwards. I just was worried that one day Jae would wake up in cold sweats behind this shit. Everybody knew that Jae still had nightmares about her parents and about the night her sister and son's father were killed. I didn't want anything else to be able to come and haunt her.

Staring at Jaeda, I felt my dick rising but I knew that I couldn't act on my urges. I knew I had to be patient due to her injuries but more so because there was a house full of people not too far away that probably wouldn't want to hear Jae calling for Jesus right about now. I sat up on my side and leaned in to kiss Jaeda on the lips. First just a peck but once I felt her lean into me, I began to kiss her vigorously as my hands roamed her body softly. I reached in between her legs and I could feel the heat radiating off of her pussy. I swear I could hear that shit calling my name.

I lowered myself to the floor and got on my knees as I pulled Jaeda towards the edge of the bed. I grabbed the waistline of her yoga pants, pulled them over her ankles and threw them on the bed. I stared straight forward at Jae's freshly waxed pussy and looked up at her. "When did you find time to get a wax?" I asked as I blew on her enlarged pearl.

"I had the lady at my salon make a house call. For an extra $150, she made a house call. You must have forgotten I'm the man around here," Jaeda said as she let out a small laugh.

I looked up at her frowning. "You better not be the man around nowhere, I need my bitch all woman," I said as I licked my tongue at her pussy. I spread her lips with my thumbs and placed her legs over my shoulders as I dove in to her warmth and staked my claim on her. I went in and feasted on her like it was the very last meal I would ever have. I needed to hear her call my name. I needed to feel her fingertips on my scalp pulling me further into her. I wanted to take her breath away and then give her those same breaths right back.

I opened my eyes and stared at Jaeda. Her love faces were sexy as fuck and I could get used to seeing them every day and every night. "Look at me, Jae," I said as I pulled her even further off of the bed and into my mouth. I dug my tongue in her as far as it could go. The way that I was eating the box, I knew that my tongue was going to be sore later on, but I had to make her feel my love by every lick and every slurp.

"Fuck. Quinton, stop!" Jaeda pushed me with her good arm but I grabbed her wrists and held them so that she couldn't control my movements. I could feel her warmth heating up and I knew that she was on the verge of releasing. Her orgasm was rising and I needed to feel it. I dove in even more aggressively and wrote my name all in it. Hell, I wrote our future kids' names in that shit. Not a second later, I felt her squirt all over my face. I didn't pull back, though. I kept up my momentum as her pussy juices coated my nose, mouth and chin. That shit was the sweetest shit I had ever tasted. Yeah, she was definitely my bitch for good. I was putting a ring on her ass and a lock on this pussy, ASAP.

"You ain't got to say it back, Jae, but I love you and one day you will understand that we were really made for each other," I said as I wiped my mouth with my hand and stood up, handing her the yoga pants that I'd removed a few minutes ago.

"There is a pack of toothbrushes in the medicine cabinet," Jae said as I helped her stand up and pull her pants up.

Chapter 17: Jaeda

My body was weak from being in the hospital for almost three weeks, so I held on to Q's arm as he helped me down the stairs into the living room. I had to have an oxygen tank at home with me at least until my next doctor's appointment. My injured lung wasn't fully healed yet so I had my moments when I needed the oxygen. I hated feeling helpless but I was grateful that I was still alive. My lungs would heal eventually and so would the strength in my arm. I had gotten used to the random feelings I would get throughout the day due to the nerve damage I'd endured. Sometimes I felt tingling and sometimes it was pure pain but I worked hard every day with various exercises to gain my strength back.

Once I got to the living room, I smiled wide as I walked into all of my family and friends sitting around clowning as usual. "I hope y'all weren't up there doing no nasty shit," Jamiya said with her nose turned up.

I shook my head and laughed. "Man, gone with that shit, J. Stay out grown folks' business," Q said as he sat down next to me and pulled my legs onto his lap.

"Well I guess that means they were doing something, nasty motherfuckers," Greg said and we all burst out laughing.

I lay my head back against the soft leather of the couch and just absorbed the energy that was around me. I loved these people and I knew that each and every one of them loved me just as much. "I just want y'all to know that I really love and appreciate all of y'all and I wouldn't trade ner' one of you for anything in the world," I said, on the verge of tears. I looked over at China and her sensitive ass was already dropping tears.

"Nigga, you done got soft. What the fuck? You must have lost that pimp portion of ya' blood after all that shit," B said, laughing.

"Bitch, fuck you. I take that back. I would trade you for a plate of macaroni and cheese right now, fool," I said, rolling my eyes at him.

"Don't get mad at us because your ass a softie now. Shit, we ain't take yo' juice," Greg said. We all laughed and I wasn't even going to say anything back because we would be going back and forth all damn day, messing with his retarded ass.

"Can we eat, shit?" Rico asked, rubbing his stomach. We all nodded our heads.

Shit, I was starving my damn self. "We can eat in here because I don't feel like moving anymore," I said, looking at China. She nodded and got up to start making plates. Her ass was so domesticated. I loved the way she just did stuff like we were all her children. Tamia got up with her and they disappeared into the kitchen.

I refused to let China cook this time so I ordered from this soul food company that catered. I had been wanting some good ass food and since I had missed being home for Thanksgiving by a couple of days, I decided to remix it so I got a pan of mac n' cheese, dressing and turkey wings with some cabbage and red velvet cake. That shit had my house smelling right and I didn't want to wait any longer to eat. I shifted slightly due to the pain shooting through my arm but I was trying to let the thought of the food hitting my taste buds overpower the pain.

"You good, Jae Money?" Gio asked, noticing my discomfort.

I squeezed my eyes shut and Q's overly dramatic ass jumped up from under my legs and was kneeled down in front of me. I opened my eyes and burst out laughing. "Nigga, what the fuck you was about to do?" I asked as I saw the look of concern on his face. I reached out and rubbed the hair on his chin. He had grown it out to a full beard and I swear he was sexy as hell. "Sucka for love ass nigga, if you would have moved any faster, my crippled ass would have been smooth on the floor. Scary ass nigga," I said, laughing.

"Well, I was worried about your big headed ass for a second but next time I know to let your ugly ass suffer and you gonna be begging for my love one day," he said as he stood up and walked towards the kitchen. I laughed because his ass was so cute.

I looked at Gio and smiled. He had been such a big brother to me. Shit, every nigga in the room had been and I figured now would be the best time to address the Lo situation. I looked around and everybody was quiet, either in their phone or having side conversations.

"Lo was the one that stabbed me. I bumped into her as she was leaving out of Denny's and you already know I got in that ass on sight, but her ass started stabbing me but now she's pregnant by Tay and I gave Jamiya the green light. Baby or not, she's done," I said quickly. I had blurted everything out so fast that I hadn't even taken a breath and it had left me kind of lightheaded. I looked up and everybody was staring at me like I had just sprouted two heads.

"So you held all of this in? Why did you wait three weeks to let us know that bitch was the one to fuck you up?" Dolo yelled angrily. I looked over at Gio and Greg and the both of them had fire in their eyes.

"Bruh, calm your ass down. I didn't really know what I wanted to do and I didn't want none of you trigger happy ass niggas to do anything until I was sure. Now that I know everything and have slept on the shit, I made my call and Jamiya will have it taken care of," I said as I picked up my phone and started to check my emails. I knew that everybody was pissed but I was positive that they would get over it soon enough.

We were all sitting in the living room eating and enjoying each other's company when my doorbell rang, I looked around wondering who the hell was at my door considering that anybody that I would have been expecting was already sitting around me. "Can you grab the door for me please, Q?" I asked, turning towards him.

He nodded his head and got up to answer the door. After a few seconds, I heard laughing in the foyer and craned my neck to see who was coming around the corner but I still couldn't see and I could only hear Q's big ass mouth as he was laughing hella hard. Once they got closer, I saw Ms. Tracy, Tone's mother. She spoke and waved to everybody as she walked over to me with tears in her eyes. She had been gone for the past couple of weeks on her honeymoon and hadn't seen me since before I went into the hospital. Yes, Ms. Tracy had gotten her groove all the way back and had found her a little boo and their asses had gone off to Hawaii and gotten married and then had the nerve to go to Bermuda for another two weeks afterwards. I was happy that she was living her life and had found her happiness even if I hadn't been there to witness the ceremony.

After Baby Tone was killed, she made it a point to call and check in on me once a week. We all loved Ms. Tracy and her husband Lou was hella cool. They had become like parents to all of us.

"Hey Ms. Tracy, how was the trip and where is Lou?" I asked as I placed my plate next to me on the coffee table and reached up to give her a hug.

"Baby, the trip was amazing and Lou's ass caught a bad cold so he stayed home, but I had to come and check in on you. I have been so worried about you but I made sure to call Gio every day for updates," she said as she then went around giving hugs to everybody and stopping to pick up Gioni's little spoiled behind.

We sat around enjoying each other's company talking and clowning until late into the night, being around everybody was like medicine to my soul.

***

I stepped off of the elevator leaving Mark's office, headed to go meet with my realtor Rafael to look at some locations for my diner. I was happy to be back in the swing of things and it felt good to be making progress with my business venture. I needed to hurry up and meet with Rafael so that I could look at these buildings and then get to the block. I hadn't been on the block much since I came home from the hospital because I had been trying to heal but now that I was feeling more like myself, I needed to go and do a pop up visit just to make my presence known. I had the Squad out there running shit but I knew that in order for everything to continue to run smoothly, I needed to be around more.

I hopped into my lavender Audi truck and pulled into traffic headed towards the first location that Rafael had sent me. I followed the navigation and was there within twenty minutes. I pulled up and called to let him know that I had arrived. Rafael let me know that he would be pulling up in five minutes. I saw that I had a message from Q so I opened it up.

Q Baby: *When I touch down tonight I hope you be ready to show ya nigga some real love, I love tasting that pussy but I'm ready to kill some shit tonight. Get sexy for Daddy, see u at 9.*

Me: *You ain't running shit, who said I was fucking you tonight?*

Q Baby: *Yeah play if you want...We know!!*

I laughed to myself as I removed my keys from the ignition. Q and I hadn't had sex since we had made it official but we had used other ways to please each other. Due to my body healing, Q had decided to wait on having sex. His conceited ass swore he was going to hurt somebody.

Rafael had just pulled up and parked right next to me so I grabbed my purse and stepped out of my truck. I walked up to Rafael and greeted him with a hug. He kissed my cheek and complimented my attire. I was dressed cute yet professionally today in a pair of tan slacks and a denim button up top with a pair of nude pumps and a matching Celine bag. I still had a bag in the backseat with a change of clothes. I wouldn't dare show up to the block dressed like this. It was literally a couple of weeks before Christmas and that is when niggas got desperate so I had to be prepared because you never knew when a nigga was going to try you on some come up shit.

Rafael ended up showing me three buildings and I ended up choosing the second one that he had shown me. I made an offer and now I would play the waiting game to see if the owner would accept or not. I was pretty sure that everything would go along smoothly so I pulled off and headed towards the hood with no worries.

I pulled up to McDonalds and grabbed my bag out of the back seat and then ran inside so that I could change and grab me some food. It was going to be a long day on the block so I knew if I didn't eat now, I probably wouldn't for the rest of the day. I looked at my watch and it was just past noon, my day had started early. I was anxious for this night to be over because I honestly couldn't wait to be laid up under Quinton. He had been gone for a week and I was missing him like crazy. We'd had talks about him making the Bay his permanent residence again but as of right now, he was back and forth until we figured it all out.

Being in a relationship with Q was different. He was attentive to my needs and sensitive to my moodiness. I knew that I was a handful but I was grateful for a man like him in my life because he really supported my dreams and pushed me to be the best that I could be. We had only been official for about a month and a half but I really could feel the difference in myself. I had played myself after Tone passed by fucking with Chris' bitch ass and then wasting my time in a relationship with Lo. Now that I was in my right mind, I was looking back on that shit so embarrassed and disappointed in myself. I was sure that my sister and Tone probably thought that I was the dumbest bitch alive. I guess everybody made mistakes but shit, I had made some very bad decisions in the past couple of years and it had cost me a lot.

I pulled up to the block and hopped out, looking around to see who was where. I spotted B's whip up the street so I pulled my phone and hit him with a text letting him know I was on the block because I didn't see his ass anywhere. I walked towards the back of the apartments that were up the street and heard a bunch of commotion.

I shook my head as I walked up and Jamiya, B, Lil Tae and a couple of the niggas were engaged in a dice game. I told this bitch Jamiya to come over this way to make sure that the safes was cleared out and this bitch was back here shooting dice with these niggas. I swear she was so damn hood. "The fuck y'all back here doing? I guess the knocks just supposed to come and serve they got damn selves, huh?" I asked, looking around at everybody. "J, did you handle that yet?" I asked.

She glanced up at me and nodded her head. "Hell yeah. Shit, I did that when I first got here but these niggas were talking a gang of shit so after I made the drops, I slid back through so I could teach these dumb ass niggas a lesson about playing with a real bitch," she said as she slid the dice out her hand real smooth like.

I just shook my head and walked off. "Whatever. You and B lame ass come holla at me when y'all done losing money," I threw over my shoulder.

"Bitch, don't jinx me. I'm up right now," Jamiya yelled back.

I walked back towards my car and grabbed a Swisher and some weed as I sat down on a crate on the sidewalk and watched the block. I pulled my ringing phone from my pocket and answered as Dolo was calling. He was in the area so I told his ass to slide through. It was cold as shit outside and the block was moving. A couple of niggas spoke and kept it pushing and all the knocks acknowledged me before they made it to the back of the apartments to cop. I knew Q was beyond ready for me to give this part of my life up and honestly, I was too but I couldn't lie and act like this shit wasn't a part of me now.

I thought back to when Laela, Sage, Jah and Tone were still alive and we used to really be out here hella deep. We were really doing numbers in the streets and being out on the block was an everyday thing. The looking over our shoulders, the fights, shootings, running from the police and just chilling and clowning was all a part of how our circle gained trust within each other. I didn't mind letting this all go to raise a family and be the woman that Q wanted me to be. Shit, the woman that I had once dreamed to be. But now I wondered if I would just be able to give this life up cold turkey. Even with the bad that came along with the streets, that fast money, the power and respect gave you a rush that was indescribable. I looked around and could see the old days clear as day but how many chances was God willing to give me before my time was finally up?

Chapter 18: Loren

I walked out of the doctor's office with tears in my eyes. My baby wasn't growing as healthy as she should have been and I was so depressed that I had to deal with this shit alone. I was pissed that Jaeda had killed my baby's daddy and I just didn't know what to do. I knew that it was my fault that my baby wasn't healthy. The social worker had come in today and talked to me about substance abuse and the effects that it was having on my child and I knew that I would have to force myself to stay sober for the rest of my pregnancy, but it was easier said than done. I was really taking Diontay's death hard as hell. I had gotten into a fight with his dumb ass baby mama on the day of his funeral because that bitch tried to flexx on me and say I wasn't allowed in the funeral. That bitch had me fucked up. Like I told her ass, I loved him and was fucking on him just like she was and the proof was evident in my baby bump. I ended up getting dragged out of the funeral and I didn't even get the chance to say my final goodbyes.

I hopped in my car and leaned my head against the steering wheel, I really just wanted to stuff my nose with some candy but I needed to really force myself to stay sober for the sake of my child. I really did want my daughter to be healthy. Even though I would be a single mother and I had no idea how my ass was about to fully support this baby, I didn't want to bring her any harm. At first I only thought about this pregnancy as a meal ticket but after feeling my child move inside of me, I began to look at it differently. Karma had definitely come around full circle on my ass because the doctor had told me that there was a 75% chance that my baby would be born with a mental disability and it was all my fault. I cried so hard that my head was now pounding so I leaned my seat back and closed my eyes right there in the parking lot of the doctor's office.

I was deep into my dream when I heard knocking. I was hella mad because I was just about to pick up Diontay from the airport in my dream. I opened my eyes and had to blink a few times so that they could adjust. I rolled down my window looking at the pretty Asian nurse named Tammy standing at my window.

"Hey, Loren, are you good? Have you been out here since your appointment?" she asked, looking down at the watch on her wrist.

I nodded my head as I rubbed my eyes and looked at the time on my car. I had been knocked out for almost four hours/ the sun had set and it was now dark outside. I instantly felt embarrassed/ I just knew she thought I was some kind of homeless junkie now.

"I'm sorry. Loren. I didn't mean to embarrass you. I was just worried. I know you just lost the father of your child so I know things are crazy right now but if you ever need anything, you can give me a call at any time," Tammy said as she passed me a business card with her cell and work number on it. I nodded my head as tears streamed down my cheeks. "Go home, Loren, and get some food and rest, honey."

I looked into her face and could tell that she was sincere, "Thank you Tammy." I said as I placed the card inside of my phone case.

I started my car and pulled out of the parking lot in the direction of my house. I was trying to stay focused but I couldn't think straight. I was torn between going to sit in front of Jaeda's house and going to cop a party pack, food and home weren't even on my mind. I hated Jaeda at this point in my life. It was all her fault that I was in this predicament. All she had to do was love me and be loyal to me like I was to her. It was because of her that my baby would grow up with no father. It was because of her that my baby was going to be born retarded. I hated her with everything in me. She was the root to all of my problems. I wasn't a gangster or a killer but I wanted to fuck her up. Had I known that she had a hand in killing my nigga, I would have killed that bitch the night I stabbed her ass at Denny's. I couldn't care less that he was the one that killed her baby's father and sister. Shit, her baby wasn't even alive anymore so what did it matter to her? I was trying my best to stay away from the drugs because I had already caused my daughter enough damage.

I found myself sitting across the street from Jaeda's house watching as her and Q were sitting in the living room playing UNO with Dolo and Tamia. She had the drapes from her bay window pulled open so that you could see her Christmas tree that stood in front of the window for the world to see. I looked up as her and Q exchanged a deep passionate kiss. I instantly felt my body heat up as he grabbed her ass and then sucked on her neck.

"Aaagh!" I yelled out in frustration as I watched her be happy with the nigga that she swore up and down she didn't want. When we were together, I had asked that bitch time and time again to just keep it real and she swore she was cool. Even before us she had offered to let me fuck with him. I had told her that I didn't like him but the few times I had tried to push up on his stuck up ass, he acted like I was some nasty bitch with the plague or something. Fuck the both of them.

I watched them for a few minutes as I ate my Big Mac and let the wheels in my head turn. They had to pay for playing me like a dumb bitch. I had something for their asses but it would take me a couple of days. I was supposed to meet up with this guy that I knew tomorrow and cop this gun from him. I had been super paranoid lately and I felt like I should get some protection, especially since in a few months I would have a baby to protect. Thoughts of killing Jaeda and Q had crossed my mind a few times but I was not sure I could really go through with it. I stayed parked in the same spot for another hour before I had seen enough and was ready to just go crash in my own bed. I started my car and drove off. It was going on midnight and I knew I needed to leave before I got spotted.

I walked in the door of my house and kicked my boots off as soon as I stepped in the living room. I plopped down on the couch and closed my eyes. I was exhausted, pissed off and emotional as hell. I let the tears fall freely from my eyes as I thought about what my life had become. I wasn't even on the couch for that long when my phone started ringing.

I let out a long sigh and looked at the screen to see that this nigga James from Brookfield that I had been spending a little time with was calling me. I thought about it for a second and answered before it went to voicemail. I had kicked it with James a few times and he was more than good in bed but he had a bigger coke habit than me and was super clingy but I kept him around because the D was A1.

I pulled myself up from the couch and walked into my bathroom in the hallway. I grabbed a wash cloth and towel from the shelf over my toilet and hopped in the shower. I had been out all day and needed to freshen up before he arrived. I hoped his ass ate already and wasn't expecting me to feed his ass. I had made him dinner once and I swear he thought that he was supposed to get it every time. I was not his bitch and my pregnant ass wasn't about to be slaving over no stove for no nigga that wasn't mine.

By the time I had finished washing myself up, I heard a knock at my front door. I hadn't even had time to put any lotion on my body. I walked through the living room and pulled my towel tighter as I opened the front door for James. He stood in the doorway looking high as hell. I shook my head and moved to the side as I let him in. He stood about six feet even and was dark skinned with long dreads that hung past his shoulder in a neat French braid. His scent was a mixture of weed and cologne. He brushed past me and stared into my face as we walked towards the couch to have a seat.

I pulled my legs up under me as he set his phone and keys on the coffee table and turned the TV on. I forgot my cable was off so I got up and turned on the PlayStation turned on Netflix and then returned to my spot on the couch.

"Where the fuck you been all damn day?" James asked as he pulled me towards him.

I looked at him and mugged a little. "I had a doctor's appointment today and that's all," I said as I lay my head back and closed my eyes. I was hoping that he would just shut up and possibly rub my swollen aching feet. "That shit don't take all damn day, Lo. I drove past this motherfucker twice tonight and you weren't here. So where the fuck you been, bruh?" he yelled, slightly pushing me off of him. I looked at him like he was crazy. This is exactly why I couldn't stand him. Sometimes he thought he was my daddy and he was far from it but especially when he was high. James threw his foot up on the coffee table and glared at me waiting for me to answer him as if my answer was going to change.

"What, James? I told you where I went and now you're telling me that you were stalking me and waiting for a new answer. You aren't my nigga and I don't owe you an explanation," I said and turned towards the television but was grabbed around the throat by his big hands.

He was squeezing the hell out of my windpipe. I was clawing at his hands and I could feel my daughter moving around frantically in my stomach as well. Tears fell from my eyes as he stared at me through red, squinted eyes. "Bitch, I don't give a fuck who you think I am but

194

you not about to be talking to me like I'm one of these lame ass niggas. Hoe, I will kill you in here bitch!" he yelled and then let my throat go.

I rubbed one hand over my sore throat and rubbed the other over my stomach to calm my daughter down. I jumped up and scooted to the other side of the couch as he went back to watching the TV like he hadn't just been squeezing the life out of me. "You need to leave," I said but it came out barely over a whisper. James didn't budge. "You need to leave!" I yelled this time.

He looked at me for a second and then turned back towards the TV again. "Girl, shut your ass up. I'm not going nowhere so unless you about to suck this dick, then shut the fuck up. Please."

I got up and walked into my room. I didn't want to be around his ignorant ass any longer. I was so exhausted that I dropped my towel and climbed into my bed butt naked. I closed my eyes and let the aroma from my candle take me away. I woke up feeling James' hands groping my ass. I scooted away from him and turned over on my back.

"So you acting funny? Now you don't want to get high with daddy?" he asked as he took out a baggy filled with coke.

I looked at him and then back at the baggy but I shook my head. I was cursing myself for even letting James come over. He hadn't even been here that long and had managed to choke me out and now he was sitting here offering me something that I was trying my hardest to stay away from.

"Bitch, I don't even know why I came over here with your funny acting ass. I should have gone to my baby mama house if you were going to be a bitch tonight," James said as he grabbed me around my waist and lifted my legs up. He dropped his pants in one swift motion and entered me roughly. I winced in pain and closed my eyes as his disrespectful ass pumped in and out of me roughly. I was praying that he would be quick but knowing that he was high as shit, I knew this bullshit could last all night.

***

I walked through the mall feeling a little down. I was getting bigger and bigger by the day but I was also getting angrier. I was pissed off as I watched the happy couples walking through the mall holding hands and giggling. This was not where I wanted to be but I needed to buy some more clothes. I had been having crazy awkward feelings lately and I really would rather be in the confinement of my own four walls, so I was trying my best to be in and out but the mall was so damn packed that it wasn't happening fast enough. It was the holiday season and Christmas was only a week away. I grabbed my bags from the chair and emptied my food tray into the garbage as I walked off out the mall towards my car.

I turned around and looked over my shoulder as a funny feeling swept over me. The sun had gone down about an hour ago and now it was dark and very chilly outside. I pulled my jacket tighter and walked as briskly as I could to my car. I grabbed my ringing phone out of my pocket and answered it. It was Tammy the nurse from my Ob-Gyn. We had gotten pretty close lately. I had been talking to her and meeting with her once or twice. She had really become a great support system to me. She was easy to talk to and she really provided a lot of positive words when I needed them.

"Hey, Tammy, what's up?" I answered as I looked over my shoulder again.

"Hey boo, I was just checking on you to see how you were feeling. Did you eat today?" I told her I had just got finished eating and she had to ask exactly what I ate. She was so determined to make sure I maintained a healthy pregnancy. "I'm leaving the mall now but you can swing by my place in like an hour or so," I said as I spotted my car and hit the locks.

"Girl, you better go straight home. I'm not about to be waiting forever for you to get there like last time," Tammy said.

I laughed. Once I made it to my car, I hopped in and strapped on my seatbelt. I sat my phone down on my chest and as soon as I stuck my key into the ignition, my driver's side door was snatched open.

"Get out the car bitch!" I looked towards the masked gunman and took a deep breath. I shook my head no. "That wasn't a yes or no question. Get the fuck out!" the gunman said again.

I looked back and there was a dark colored van parked directly behind my car with the sliding door open. I could hear Tammy yelling through the phone but I was frozen and couldn't muster up the courage to grab it and hang it up. I didn't want her to worry but I knew she could hear what was transpiring. I knew I had no choice but to comply so I unstrapped my seatbelt and moved to get out, the gunman grabbed my arm and pulled me but the seatbelt was tangled in my crossover bag and it tugged me back to where my back hit the car roughly. "Let's go!" he said as they snatched me again successfully and stuffed me in the van. My phone dropped and slid under my car somewhere. Once I was inside, another masked gunman blindfolded me and then pushed me onto the back row of seats.

Tears ran down my face as I lay on the backseat. I didn't know what was about to happen to me. Shit, I didn't even know why it was happening to me but all I wanted was to be able to protect my child. After a few minutes, I felt the van come to a halt. The sliding door opened and I was snatched out and put on my feet. My back was killing me and my baby was doing somersaults in my stomach but I kept moving as I was being dragged along on the ground beneath my feet. We stopped after taking a couple of steps up on what I assumed was a porch. Once I heard the door open, I was pushed inside and forced onto a couch. "Shut the fuck up crying! Damn!" the masked gunman to the right of me said. I knew that voice from somewhere but I couldn't place it. It was rough but I couldn't think of who it could be.

As soon as I started to relax a little, I started being attacked. I could feel a few different fists as well as feet on me as my body was being bruised and split open. I tried my best to ball up and cover my stomach as to not let my baby be hurt. I began to scream and cry because I couldn't believe that I was putting my baby through so much pain and suffering and she wasn't even here yet. I could feel everything in me giving up. My body was shutting down and I had no more to give. I could feel myself blacking out and I couldn't hold on any longer. I said a quick prayer for my daughter and me and then everything faded to black.

I jumped up as I felt cold water splashing over my body. It took me a minute to realize that my eyes weren't blindfolded anymore. I squinted a little as my eyes adjusted to where I was. The smell was the same as when I first was brought in and thrown on the couch so I knew that I was in the same spot. I didn't know how long I had been unconscious but it seemed to be still dark outside so

I knew it hadn't been too long. I looked up and was staring into the faces of Jaeda's cousin Jamiya, her friend Pam and Izz's crazy ass. Once I saw these three faces, I knew that I would not be leaving alive. Tears immediately fell from my eyes. I couldn't believe this is what my life had come to.

"Oh no, boo. Don't start shedding tears now. Were you crying when you were stabbing my cousin? Or when you were fucking on the enemy? Or how about when you were sitting outside my cousin's house night after night? Or even when you bought this gun?" Jamiya was inching closer and closer to me and I could feel my heart rate speeding up and my breathing going ragged. I knew this was the end.

I shook my head. "What about my baby?" I asked, hoping to save our lives somehow.

Jamiya started laughing as she looked back at Izz and Pam. "Aye, Izz, this hoe think somebody cares about her or her seed by that bitch ass nigga Tay. Ha!" she said as they all began to laugh.

I shook my head because out of all the people in Jaeda's crew, I knew that these three didn't give two fucks about me and my child and that's why Jaeda had probably sent them. They were young and reckless and were moving in the streets with no heart. Izz grabbed me by my arm and forcefully pushed me down on the floor. My stomach hit the floor first and I was hit with a horrible pain that went through my abdomen and back. As soon as I realized I was lying on a large rug, Pam had leaned down and placed duct tape over my mouth and the rug was being rolled up with me in it I could hear the duct tape as they continued to roll me in the rug. They were taping up the rug.

I closed my eyes as I felt myself being lifted from the ground and being carried back outside and thrown back into the van. My body felt as if it had been hit by a few semi-trucks. I was crying so hard because I just wanted to die but I wanted my child to live. I knew something was wrong because I could feel warm moisture between my legs and the movement in my belly had ceased.

After a few minutes of driving, I was being pulled out of the van yet again but I could hear the loud sound of traffic all around me, I didn't understand where I was or where I was being taken to. I tried to wiggle around as much as I could through the unbearable pain as I could feel myself being lifted into the air. I began to panic as I realized we were somewhere on the freeway. I could barely make out what was being said around me until I heard Izz counting to three. As soon as he said three, I could feel my body being hoisted and thrown over some kind of railing. My body was falling fast and I could hear cars honking around me.

"Jesus!" I yelled as my body was smacked by a car and then thrown across the freeway, landing on the pavement. I could hear cars around me but they were starting to sound far away. I knew my child was already dead and I could feel the life slipping away from my body as well. This time I welcomed death. I had nothing to live for.

Chapter 19: Big Money Q

I pulled up to Jaeda's house and got out, grabbing the bags of groceries that I had just picked up from the store. It was Christmas Eve and Jaeda had asked me to help her cook Christmas dinner. We were making gumbo but we were also going to make some desserts. I had grabbed some egg nog and Hennessey so that we could cake up and watch *A Christmas Story* later on.

I pulled out my keys and walked into the house. I could hear Jaeda's ass in the kitchen with the music blasting. I could tell she had already started the gumbo because I could smell the aroma and that shit was smelling right. "Honey. I'm home!" I said, walking up on her. I placed my hands around her waist and nuzzled my face into her neck as I inhaled her perfume. I loved the hell out of this girl and I couldn't wait to spend the rest of my life with her.

"It's about time, nigga. Where yo' ass been? Taking all got damn day with the stuff," she said as I grabbed her ass and kissed her cheek. She turned towards me and looked into my eyes.

"Fuck you staring at? Better watch that food before you mess some shit up," I said as I pecked her lips.

"Boy, knock it off. I know what I'm doing."

I winked my eye at her and walked out of the kitchen. I walked to the hall closet and placed the bags that I had snuck in the house on the very top shelf behind the piles of bedding. I had taken a trip to the jewelry store today and copped some shit but I knew I needed to put it up somewhere that Jaeda's nosey ass wouldn't look. She had said she didn't want shit for Christmas but I had caught her ass snooping in random spots around the house for the past couple of weeks. Every time I called her out on it her retarded ass told me she had seen ants and was making sure there weren't anymore, but I haven't seen one ant or can of ant spray or nothing.

I have been telling her slick ass that I didn't buy her anything because she told me not to. I couldn't wait until tomorrow morning to see her face when she woke me up and I told her I didn't get her shit. I was about to sleep good tonight and sleep late through the morning. This shit wasn't nothing special. We didn't have any kids to wake up with and dinner didn't start until late afternoon so Jae better gone with all that extra shit. Her spoiled ass will most definitely be mad as hell for a minute but once she saw my gifts later on, I was sure she would be good.

I walked into Jaeda's bathroom and turned the shower on. It was funny because whenever I was out here, I hardly ever stayed at my own house. I always found myself here at Jaeda's spot. I stripped down and stared into the mirror as I waited for the water to heat up. I couldn't believe that I was really at the point of settling down. Yeah, I had been in a relationship with Laniece for a minute but even throughout that, I never felt like giving up all my hoes and committing only to her. Jaeda, though. She was it for me. Everything about her was the truth and I needed that to be all me, period. I stepped into the shower thinking about the steps that I was taking to secure our future. I said a short prayer in the shower to ensure that God was behind me all the way. I looked up just as Jaeda was stepping in the shower.

I licked my lips as I eyed Jaeda's body hungrily. Even with the various scars that covered her body due to the many horrific events that she had endured, she was still the most beautiful female to me and for her to finally be all mine had my dick rock hard. "What you doing in here? I thought you were cooking," I said.

She smiled at me and placed her index finger to her lips. "Shhh," she said as she dropped to her knees and placed her warm mouth around my shit. She licked around the tip for a minute before taking it all down as far as it would go. I swear Jae had a platinum mouth. Her head game was A1 and I would kill a nigga trying to push up on my shit. I took a step back as she continued to deep throat my shit. I put my head back and squeezed my eyes closed as I let the feeling of pure satisfaction take over my body. "Fuck, baby, get that shit. It's almost there," I said as she started going crazy, slurping and sucking the hell out of me. This right here was life. "Fuck!" I moaned as I released down her throat. She sucked me dry and I couldn't even move to finish my shower. I stood in the same spot for a moment before I felt Jaeda washing me up. She knew how to treat a nigga like a king. She always kept my balls empty, stomach full and mind off of bullshit, so all I needed now was for her to let the streets go.

After we were both clean, we stepped out of the shower and threw on some loungewear before returning to the kitchen to finish Christmas dinner. "Thanks, baby," I said as I smacked her ass.

"Nigga, don't ever thank me for head. That's just weird," she said as she scrunched up her nose. I laughed at her crazy ass because she was serious as hell. She was weird her damn self, but had a long ass list of shit that she didn't like because it was weird.

"Ha, ha. Don't flatter yourself. I meant thanks for taking a chance on a nigga and just being you, but that head is official, though," I said as I winked at her.

She shook her head and swatted at me. "Yeah. Okay. Quinton." She was so difficult. Her ass didn't know how to express her feelings in words but I was glad her actions spoke for her.

I walked to the counter, grabbing items out of the grocery bags and we proceeded to get to work. I refused to be up all damn night cooking for these niggas when I had pussy I was trying to get into. I eyed Jaeda's ass in her leggings and that was all the motivation I needed to get a move on.

The next morning, I woke up to Jaeda waking me up with kisses on my chest. I opened my eyes and stared into hers as she smiled brightly at me. "Why you up all early, girl?" I asked her as I snatched her up and pulled her on top of me.

"It's Christmas and I wanted to give you your gifts."

I looked at the time on the cable box and shook my head. "Babe, it's not even eight yet. You couldn't let a nigga sleep in and then give it to me, especially after all that shit you was doing to me last night?" I asked, thinking back to our love session last night as I kissed her lips and then shifted her off of me so that I could get up and relieve myself. Jaeda followed me to the bathroom and stood in the doorway as I stood over the toilet.

"Sorry, baby, I guess I got a little too juiced but now that you are up, aren't you ready to see what I got you?" she asked.

"Sure, bae, give me a second." Once she walked away, I flushed the toilet and then washed my face and brushed my teeth. I didn't know what her sneaky ass had gotten me as a gift but she was a shopaholic and was always shopping online so there's no telling what her ass had paid for.

Once I was done handling my hygiene, I walked down to Jae's living room and she was sitting on the edge of the couch texting on her phone. I laughed because she looked so anxious and it was funny because she wasn't even the holiday spirit type. She had been dreading the holiday arrival for weeks and now she was sitting on the edge of the couch tapping her foot impatiently.

"Bruh, I'm going to need your ass to calm the hell down," I said as she hopped up and grabbed my arm, pulling me towards the garage. I let Jaeda lead me into the garage and over to the side of her truck. There was the cleanest black and blue Yamaha YZF-R1M with a matching helmet. My mouth dropped open because I had been looking at this damn bike for a few months but had yet to actually go about purchasing it.

"Damn, babe! I ain't going to lie. You got me speechless. Thanks, baby," I said as I kissed her and then ran my hand over the seat and handlebars. The shit was clean as fuck and I couldn't wait to hop on it and test it out.

Jaeda stood there watching me as I drooled over my new toy. "I hope you don't think this is it," she said with one eyebrow raised. I looked at her wondering what else she could have possibly gotten me. Again, she grabbed my arm and I followed her back through the house and into the guest room. Once we walked into the room, there was a tall reptile tank. I walked closer to it and there was a small veiled chameleon inside.

I smiled at Jaeda because she had really outdone herself. "Thank you, babe, this shit is nice," I said as I turned towards her and wrapped her in my arms, kissing her deeply. I loved this girl because no matter how short of a time we had been together, she didn't hold out on a nigga. She went hard for me like I went hard for her and that's what I liked and what I needed. "I'm going to name him Jaeda," I said as I tapped her lightly on the ass.

"Nigga, you better not name that ugly motherfucker after me!" she yelled, giving me the evil eye. I laughed because she was dead serious.

We walked out of the guest room and walked back into Jae's bedroom and both sat down on the bed. I closed my eyes as I lay back on the bed and placed my arms behind my head. I could feel Jaeda's eyes on me but I didn't budge. I was about to make her ass sweat.

"Nigga, I know you feel me staring at your ugly ass!" Jae yelled as she slapped my chest roughly.

My eyes popped open as I stared at her. "Girl, you better keep your hands to yourself before I whoop your ass. You not 100% so I suggest you be cool," I said as I sat up and leaned towards her.

She looked at me with a mean mug on her face. "So you really didn't get me shit, Quinton?" she asked, pouting.

I shook my head. "Nah, man. You said you didn't want anything but now your ass think that because you copped me some nice shit that I'm supposed to magically have a gift for you? Nah, my nigga, say what you mean and mean what you say. Next time don't say you don't want shit," I said, getting up and heading in the bathroom to take a shower.

***

Jaeda's house was full of activity as everybody sat around drinking and having a good time. We had ate about an hour ago and now we were just chilling. Charlie and Jahlisa were sitting in the middle of the floor playing with their toys and baby Gioni was asleep on Ms. Tracy's lap. Everybody was there and a couple of days ago, we got a surprise and Lexis had gotten released. It was a good thing that Jae had a big house because we were deep up in here. There were gifts over to the side that we had all received from one another and opened. I still hadn't given Jae her gifts but I planned on doing that now.

I got up and walked upstairs to the hall closet and grabbed the gift bags from the top shelf. I walked back into the living room and everybody was still chilling. I was sure they barely even noticed I had gotten up. I walked back over to Jaeda with the bags in my hands and sat down.

"Here this old sucker for love ass nigga go, about to do some light skinned nigga shit," Dolo said, laughing hella hard.

"Fuck you, nigga. Let me have my fucking moment, shit," I said as Jaeda turned towards me and everybody else turned their attention towards us as well. I shook my head because I didn't know how I was going to say what I wanted to say in this big group of clowns. These niggas stayed on play time.

I grabbed the first bag and pulled out a long jewelry box and I saw Jae's eyes sparkle. Her ass was so damn spoiled. I opened the box and her eyes began to water. I pulled the bracelet from the box and grabbed her arm to place it around her wrist. I twisted it around so that she could see all of the details. "I wanted to give you things this year that would be memorable to you considering that this is our first year together as a couple. No matter how many years go by, I know that your son will always be the most important person to you so I got three charms on this bracelet to represent Baby Tone." The first one was his birthstone which was an aquamarine heart that was surrounded by a 14 karat gold plate, the second charm was a gold letter "A" and the final piece was a gold Celtic charm that symbolized the mother and male child.

"The other three charms represent our relationship," I said, looking into her eyes as she was wiping the tears away. I looked around and all the cry baby ass females were shedding tears. The first charm was a ram head connected to a doe head with the words "His One" behind the ram and "Her Only" engraved behind the doe, the second charm was a king's crown which had a few black diamonds added in and the final charm was a queen's crown with pink diamonds. I looked up after explaining each piece and Jaeda looked like she had just cried a river. I laughed at her soft ass because she always appeared to be so tough. I pulled the second bag out and pulled out a second jewelry box.

"Damn, nigga, you got us looking bad. Shit, the rest of us going to have to go out and buy more gifts tomorrow to catch up to you, Cupid," Greg said like he was really frustrated. We all laughed.

I grabbed Jaeda's hand and looked into her eyes. "These last two gifts are a token of my love and appreciation. I take our relationship very seriously and I wanted to show you just how much. I fell in love with you the very first day that I met you that Fourth of July three years ago and I always knew that you were the one for me, so this ring is a promise that maybe not now but one day soon, I will make you my wife," I said as I pulled a solid gold 24k ring with a diamond encrusted infinity symbol. "This last and final gift," I said as I grabbed Jae's hand and placed the ring on her finger as she kissed me deeply. I kissed her just as deep because what I felt for her was just that real. I pulled the last jewelry box from the bag as I dropped Jaeda's hand.

"Damn, nigga, we might as well leave because we all about to be in the dog house with all these gifts you popping out. Light skinned niggas always got to do the most," B said as he threw his empty cup at me. These niggas were tripping but I had spent a lot of money to make sure that Jae was happy this Christmas and I could give a fuck what anybody said. Those niggas better step they grown man game up.

"This last and final gift, like I was saying before these weak ass niggas interrupted my spill, is a key to our future. I purchased us a home in Vegas, which will be our residence at the beginning of the year. I wanted to invest in our future, a new start for the new year because ain't shit in Oakland and I know that we both have business out here but in order to give this a fair chance and fresh start, I want it to be away from all the bad memories that you have here," I said, looking into her eyes.

I couldn't really read her expression, though. I knew she was thinking about everything that she had going on here but it was time for her to grow up and leave the streets alone. She had a nigga ready to give her the world and shit but was scared to scoot over and let me take the reins.

"Bitch, you better go ahead and leave with yo' nigga. Ain't shit out here and you can hop on a flight anytime. It's only 90 minutes away, bitch. Bye," Lex said, waving Jaeda off.

"You feel me?" Tamia said, high fiving Lexis. They were too damn much. I laughed because it was nice to have her back. Jizz had held her down throughout her whole bid and I was glad that Jae had her best friend back for good. You can't ever hold a real one down and Lex was as real as it got. Shit, everybody in this room was.

I looked into Jae's face and she smiled and nodded her head. "You right, Q. Ain't shit out here. I'm ready to leave this motherfucker anyway," she said as she waved her hand around for emphasis. She leaned in and pecked my lips and once she pulled back, she slapped me upside my head.

"Damn, Jae. What you do that for?" I asked as I rubbed the back of my head.

"That was for making me mad today, thinking that you really didn't get me shit!" she said. Everybody laughed because her ass could be so extra at times. "That's a good look, bruh. You better not fuck up because that's little sis and no matter how cool we are, I don't play over Jae Money," Gio said and I nodded my head.

"Aight then, Big Money. I see you, nigga, sucka ass nigga!" Rico yelled raising his double cup in the air. I laughed and raised my own cup as did everybody else.

"Let's toast to the Squad, family and more money," Dolo said as we all agreed and sipped from our cups. We kicked back and enjoyed the holiday for the rest of the night and I had never felt happier than I did now, surrounded by my girl and the people I considered my family.

Chapter 20: Dolo

I walked out of the house in my infamous all black. It was New Year's Eve and while I should have been out partying, I had things to do before I could kick back and party. I had just gotten back in town from San Diego, or Daygo as we called it. I had been out there for the past couple of days. I had finally accepted the fact that a nigga had a baby on the way. It may not have been the best of situations and it definitely wasn't with a bitch that I ever thought I would have been having a child with but I had planted the seed and I was a real nigga so I put everything to the side and stepped up like a man to take care of my responsibilities.

I had gone out there to accompany Ney to her doctor's appointment. She was going to find out the sex of the baby and wanted me to come so I did the right thing and hopped on a flight to go with her ugly ass to the doctor. Don't get me wrong. I may have been on my grown man shit but I did not ride with Ney there and I waited a few minutes so by the time I went in, she would already be in the back and I wouldn't have to be seen with her. I didn't know if I could ever get comfortable with her looks. I was ready to step up and take care of my daughter. Yeah, it's a girl. God was definitely punishing me for all the hoes I dogged in the past, but I wasn't ready to claim this Celie from *The Color Purple* looking ass bitch. She had a fat ass but her grill was disrespectful.

I hopped in the mobby and placed my gun in my lap as I looked around the car and spoke to Jamiya, Izz and Pam. I had been fucking with them and doing little plays here and there trying to get my money right. I had money and shit, plus Q and my businesses were doing well but it was different when you had another life to think about. The shit I had been doing was all for myself but now I had a daughter to do it for so I had hopped back in the trenches just to get my money up but I can't lie and say the thrill of being back in the streets didn't push me to keep doing what I was doing. Jamiya and I had been rocking these plays for a few weeks.

She had called me and told me to strap up and she was headed to get me. So, with no questions asked, I masked up and grabbed my bitch and now we were on our way. I fucked with them the long way and although I really only did dirt with Q and Rico I had to admit that Jamiya had a team of real live wires that was ready to go on call. We had been hitting all kinds of shit the last few weeks and I almost forgot how good it felt to run up on some shit. Q really didn't do shit nowadays that required too much muscle but these little motherfuckers knew where it was at and was ready to get it at all costs.

I listened as Izz ran down the play and once he was done, I pulled a blunt from behind my ear and lit it so that I could get my mind right. I bobbed my head to Future's "Colossal" and thought about the task at hand. We all had to be on point because at any given moment anything could go wrong and I didn't have time to be taking any losses. After another twenty minutes of driving, I felt the car come to a halt and everybody shifted out of their thoughts and began checking their guns. I made sure to grab my old faithful. Even though I was on some legit shit, I always kept a banger on me but when I went out to work, my .40 with the 30 was always my go to tool.

"So Izz and Pam, y'all take up the front and Dolo and I will pull up the back. There's only one nigga in there but you never know what could happen, so keep ya' eyes and ears open, feel me?"

We all hopped out of the mobby and pulled our masks down over our faces; I gripped my banger and took off across the street. There was a tall fence surrounding the house so when Jamiya and I got to the back, I did something I hadn't done in a few years and hopped that bitch. I hadn't hopped a fence since I was about 21 running from 5-0. Once I had gotten to the other side, I looked back and Jamiya's ass had some bolt cutters in her hand that she used to cut a hole in the gate large enough to squeeze through.

"Why the hell you ain't say shit before I hopped that tall ass shit, nigga?" I asked her ass while she was laughing like shit was funny.

"Man, yo' ugly ass hopped that bitch so fast I figured you needed the work out," she said as she slid past me and walked up to the back door. "This new school, baby. We make a way before we pull up. You better get with it, OG," she said as she waited by the door with her ear to it. Soon as we heard a loud bang, I kicked it in and we came through the kitchen, guns drawn. I could hear Izz's voice as we got closer to the front of the house. He had a short, dark skinned nigga by the collar with his gun raised to his forehead and Pam was tearing through the couch cushions with a knife.

"Where that shit at, my nigga? What you trying to save that shit for? It ain't even yours. Shit, you can't even get in trouble 'cus you ain't going to be around for the backlash but if you just give the shit up then you can die quick and painless but if your dirty ass want to play hard, I can make you suffer. Now which one will it be, fuck boy?"

I looked up and Jamiya had hit the kitchen, ransacking the refrigerator and the cabinets. "Bingo, we got some boy and some soft!" she yelled as she grabbed about eight boxes of waffles from the freezer that were filled with bricks of heroin and cocaine.

"Alright, pussy. Now where that paper at? You better get to talking before I run out of patience," he said as he shot the nigga in both of his knee caps.

"Aagh! Shit, Aight, man. Fuck this. Just kill me, bitch. That shit in the oven, man. It's like a soft thirty in the oven and there's a safe in the back but ain't much in there because they emptied it earlier for the re-up. Fuck! The safe already open. I never closed it back because y'all bust in this motherfucker before I had a chance," he said through clenched teeth as he squeezed his eyes from the pain, he had his hands under him and it looked like he was fumbling with something.

"Now was that so hard, bitch?" Pam said as she walked up to him and put one right between his eyes.

I walked over to him and kicked his body over. Under him was his cell phone. The nigga had made a call and it had been going for the past three minutes. I threw the phone on the floor and stomped it into pieces. "Fuck, this nigga done called somebody. We got to do it moving out this bitch," I said as we all started moving around, gathering whatever cash and drugs and we were out of there. We had all ran out of the back door.

Once everybody got through the gate, we all ran across the street and hopped in the car. Izz started the engine and pulled out onto the street. Soon as we passed up the house, another car was passing us. We sped past them but they must have been who he had called because the driver of the car busted a U-turn and sped after us. I turned around as soon as the passenger began busting shots out of the window. Pam and I both pulled our bangers and started busting back. The car began to speed up and had pulled up to the side of us. The driver then swerved over and rammed the side of our car with the driver side of their car. After regaining control, Izz sped up and I let off a few more shots. They returned shots and I ducked down as Izz hopped on the freeway and started doing it, moving on their ass in and out of lanes.

"We lost them, everybody good?" Jamiya yelled from the front of the car.

I lifted my head and my arm was on fire. "Fuck, I think that I got hit in my arm," I said as I pulled my hand back. I looked at it and it was covered in blood. "Yeah, I for damn sure got hit," I said again as I looked at Pam. She was slumped over in her seat.

"Oh shit, Pam! Fuck, Pam, look at me baby. You good?" I asked as I grabbed her and pulled her onto my lap. Jamiya turned around in her seat and started panicking. I felt her neck for a pulse and there was a very weak one. I could feel myself getting light headed but I needed to stay alert.

"Dolo, give me your banger. Izz, pull over so we can get rid of these bitches," I heard Jamiya say but she was starting to sound distant. She grabbed everybody's guns and hopped out. After a few seconds, she hopped back in but shit was starting to fade away. I could tell that I was losing a lot of blood and I was losing consciousness just as fast. Damn, man. This was what came with being in the streets. After the allure of the fast life and fast money came the griminess of your actions. You don't think about your casket when you out there trying to get it. This was what happened when you were in love with the streets. You could love the hood all day but it would never love you back.

Join our mailing list to get a notification when Leo Sullivan Presents has another release!

Text LEOSULLIVAN to 22828 to join!

To submit a manuscript for our review, email us at leosullivanpresents@gmail.com

Coming Soon from Sullivan Productions!

LEO SULLIVAN PRESENTS

Thuggin In NYC

JACORI

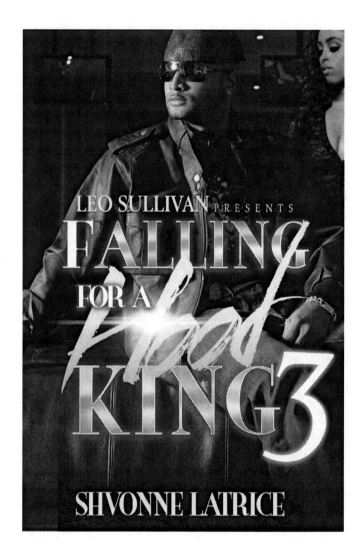

CPSIA information can be obtained at www.ICGtesting.com
Printed in the USA
LVOW06s1926251215

467864LV00022B/493/P